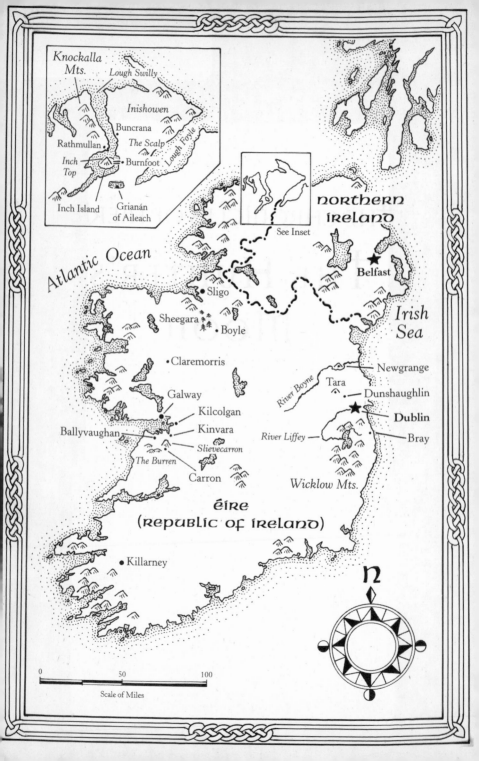

Knockalla Mts.
Lough Swilly
Inishowen
Buncrana
Rathmullan
The Scalp
Inch Top
Burnfoot
Lough Foyle
Inch Island
Grianán of Aileach

Atlantic Ocean

See Inset

NORTHERN IRELAND

★ **Belfast**

Irish Sea

• Sligo

Sheegara

• Boyle

• Claremorris

River Boyne
Tara
Newgrange
Dunshaughlin

Galway
Kilcolgan
Kinvara
Ballyvaughan
Slievecarron
The Burren
Carron

★ **Dublin**
River Liffey
Bray

Wicklow Mts.

**ÉIRE
(REPUBLIC OF IRELAND)**

• Killarney

0   50   100

Scale of Miles

N

Come away, O human child!
To the waters and the wild
With a faery, hand in hand,
For the world's more full of weeping
than you can understand

"The Stolen Child"
W. B. Yeats

THE CHRONICLES OF FAERIE

The Hunter's Moon

O.R. Melling

Amulet Books • New York

PUBLISHER'S NOTE: This is a work of fiction. Names, characters, places, and incidents are either the product of the author's imagination or are used fictitiously, and any resemblance to actual persons, living or dead, business establishments, events, or locales is entirely coincidental.

Library of Congress Cataloging-in-Publication Data:
Melling, O. R.
The Hunter's Moon / O.R. Melling.
p. cm.—(The chronicles of Faerie)
Summary: Two teenage cousins, one Irish, the other from the United States, set out to find a magic doorway to the Faraway Country, where humans must bow to the little people.
ISBN 978-0-8109-5857-0
[1. Magic—Fiction. 2. Fairies—Fiction. 3. Leprechauns—Fiction. 4. Witches—Fiction. 5. Cousins—Fiction 6. Ireland—Fiction.] I. Title II. Series: Melling, O. R. Chronicles of Faerie.
PZ7.M51625Hu 2005
[Fic]—dc22
2004022216
Paperback ISBN 978-0-8109-9214-6

First published by Amulet Books in hardcover, 2005
Copyright © 2006 O.R. Melling

Permissions
Quotation on page 36 is from *Lady Wilde's Ancient Legends of Ireland,* first published in 1888, reprinted in 1971 by O'Gorman Ltd. Galway, Ireland, and used with the kind permission of the publisher. Various verses appear in the book. Any not listed below were written by the author:
Pages 16 and 123-124: "The Gypsy Rover," traditional (with variations by the author)
Page 44: "The Rocky Road to Dublin," traditional
Page 46: "Molly Malone," traditional
Pages 257-258 and 270-271: "*Éist, A Stór,*" by Máire Breatnach, from the CD *Coinnle na nAingeal/Angels' Candles,* used with the kind permission of the singer/songwriter.

There are quotes in the book from the King James version of the Bible. These are in italics.

Designed by Jay Colvin

Published in 2009 by Amulet Books, an imprint of ABRAMS. All rights reserved. No portion of this book may be reproduced, stored in a retrieval system, or transmitted in any form or by any means, mechanical, electronic, photocopying, recording, or otherwise, without written permission from the publisher. Amulet Books and Amulet Paperbacks are registered trademarks of ABRAMS.

Printed and bound in U.S.A.
10 9 8 7 6 5 4 3

Amulet Books are available at special discounts when purchased in quantity for premiums and promotions as well as fundraising or educational use. Special editions can also be created to specification. For details, contact specialmarkets@hnabooks.com or the address below.

ABRAMS

THE ART OF BOOKS SINCE 1949

115 West 18th Street
New York, NY 10011
www.abramsbooks.com

In memory of Bernie Morris, me oul flower,
wish you could be here for this.

Acknowledgments

Many thanks to so many for their support: my daughter Findabhair; my mother Georgie and the Whelan family; John Duff and Brian Levy (dear friends in New York); Rachel Gallagher (fellow ambler and writer); Michael Scott; Joe Murray; Dr. Nena Hardie; Frank Golden and Eve Golden-Woods; Charles de Lint; Breege and Paddy McCrory of Inch Island; the Arbuckle-Brady clan (formerly of *Meitheal*); Sheila Delaney-Herceg; Maureen Galligan, Professor Dáibhí O'Cróinín and clan; Piers Dillon-Scott (webmaster); agents Lynn and David Bennett of Transatlantic Literary Inc.; the Tyrone Guthrie Center at Annaghmakerrig; all at Abrams, especially my editor Susan Van Metre; and last but not least, *Na Daoine Maithe* for their permission and assistance. *Go raibh míle maith agaibh.*

THE CHRONICLES OF FAERIE

THE HUNTER'S MOON

PROLOGUE

The muddy waters of the Liffey flowed sluggishly along the stone-walled quays. Like a weary old man in a dirty brown coat, the river wended its way through the noise and grime of Dublin City.

"Have you forgotten how to sing?" whispered the dark-eyed young man who leaned over the railings of the Ha'penny Bridge. His sloe-black eyes went darker still as he pondered the ancient river. "When we called you *Rurthach* you purled like a young stream. What have they done to you?"

A shudder passed through him as he regarded his surroundings. Concrete walls and the glare of glass towered over busy streets and traffic. In the crowds, dirty-faced children and the ragged homeless begged for money.

How could they live this way?

He turned to leave, eager to complete his mission and be gone from there, when he took pity on the river. A ray of gold flashed from his fingers to strike the turbid waters like a shaft of light. It was only for a second, the blink of an eye, but in that moment the river ran free. The young man was already hurrying from the bridge when the clear rushing waters sang their brief song.

The King passed by. Long live the King.

He came to a secondhand bookshop and café. The Winding Stair Bookroom was a Victorian brick building with a wooden front painted green and mustard-yellow. High arched windows overlooked the river. He hesitated before entering. Human meeting places made him uneasy. Once inside, the scent of old books soothed him. The musty solitude was reminiscent of a forest glade. Narrow winding stairs led upward through rooms filled with books. The upper stories had booths and tables where tea and cakes were served.

He found her on the third floor, seated by the window. She was reading a letter. Lit up by sunlight, the golden-brown hair fell over her face like a veil. A young girl, almost a woman, she was dressed in the fashion of urban youth—black sweater, black skirt, black stockings and boots. Silver earrings dangled to her shoulders.

Having found her through dreams, he was caught off guard by her reality. Mortal beauty always surprised him. While it wouldn't change his plans, he brooded a moment upon what must be done.

Unaware that she was being observed, the young woman smiled to herself as she read.

Dear Findabhair,

Gawd, your name is impossible to spell. I have to look at it twice every time I write it. You're a witch for not letting me call you Finn any more. But hey, forget the complaints, I'm coming over at last! YAHOO! Mom and Dad are forking out the fare (I'm not proud) and I've saved every dollar I could.

We're still traveling around Ireland, right? You haven't changed your mind? Don't fall in love with anyone before I get there or something stupid like that. I don't want any third parties tagging along.

Ignore that last part. Insecurity attack. Can't wait to see you. I'm packing already. Tell Aunt Pat to get in some skim milk. I'm on a diet again. (It's a losing battle. Wait till you see me, I'm a real porker.) And no hairy bacon, please! See you soon.

Luv'n'stuff,
Your cuz,
Gwen xxx

"May I sit down?"

Findabhair was about to point out archly that there were plenty of empty tables, when she looked up. The words died in her throat. He was exactly her idea of a stunning young man. His jet-black hair was pulled back in a ponytail, accenting sharp elegant features that made her think of a hawk. His eyes were dark and keen. Like

her, he favored black clothes, and she admired the quirk-
iness of the silken jacket with jeans. He seemed vaguely
familiar, though she couldn't think where she might have
seen him before.

"Do I know you?"

"Perhaps. Or you may be remembering the future.
That's possible, you know. Déjà vu."

It was a fascinating idea, as well as a good line. She
beamed a smile as he sat down.

"I brought you a gift."

The slim volume of poetry was bound in green
leather, its title stamped with gold lettering.

The Wyrd of the White Lady.

Findabhair's eyes widened.

"That's my name! Well, a translation of it. *Fionn-
abhair*. 'Fair spirit.' 'White lady.' What a brilliant coincidence!"

"There is no such thing as coincidence."

She was already turning the pages. Crisp and
browned with age, each leaf contained a poem. When she
came to one entitled "Fionavar," she let out a cry.

"There it is again! I prefer the Old Irish spelling and
I pronounce it 'finn-ah-veer' but it's the same name.
Where did you—?"

"There's no time."

An urgency had crept into his voice that made her look
around for some hidden danger. He pointed to the poem.

"Read."

Enjoying the odd encounter, she didn't stop to question him but read out loud.

Be fleet of foot,
O fair Hunted One,
From the dark of the shadow
Across the clear sun.

Like a deer on the plain,
Like a trout in the stream,
Take flight from life's bane,
To the Land of the Dream.

Come to the Sídhe-mound under the hill,
Come to the Country ruled by my will.

Caught up in the words, she didn't notice his interest in her cousin's letter that lay on the table between them. Nor did she see the hungry look enter his eyes as he read it.

"Another one?" he murmured.

"It's lovely," Findabhair said when she had finished the poem. "A bit like Yeats' 'Stolen Child.'"

"Do you know what a *Sídhe*-mound is?"

"Of course. I speak Irish. It's a fairy hill."

"Will you meet me there?"

He stood up to leave.

"What! Meet you where?"

The edge in her voice surprised her. She didn't want him to go.

He leaned toward her. She thought he was going to kiss her, but he brushed his lips against her ear.

"Tara," he whispered. "Come to Tara."

Then he was gone.

A strange gloom settled over Findabhair. She rubbed her forehead and looked around her. What was she doing? She stared out the window, across the river. A dark figure stood on the Ha'penny Bridge. He suddenly looked up at her and his glance struck her like an arrow. She shivered. Who was he? And why was he staring at her? As he disappeared into the crowd, she returned to her cousin's letter. Then she realized she had already finished reading it.

"Lost in a daydream," she muttered to herself.

She spotted the little book on the table. Caught by the title, she opened it pensively. The poems were the sort she liked, about magic and romance and the Celtic Twilight. One was entitled with a version of her name! Though she hadn't intended to buy anything, she brought the book up to the counter.

"How much is this?"

The young man at the register had bright red hair shaved on both sides of his head. His ears, nose, and eyebrow were pierced with tiny silver rings.

"It's not ours. Didn't you bring it in with you? A nice antique."

Confused by a vague memory of someone giving it to her, Findabhair laughed with embarrassment.

"Oh yeah, it is mine. Sorry, I'm feeling kind of weird today."

"You too?" The redhead grinned. "Do you know, I've had two people try to tell me they saw the Liffey running wild and clear. What do you make of that?"

"Too much sun?"

"That's what it is. And we're going to have a *fantastic* summer by the looks of things."

"Yes, I think we will," she agreed softly.

Tucking the book into her handbag, she left the shop.

One

G wen Woods stood shyly in the doorway of her cousin's bedroom. It was like peering into Aladdin's cave. The walls and windows were draped with gauzy veils that cast dappled color into the room. Posters of *The Lord of the Rings* shared space with dreamlike landscapes of other worlds. Shelves were crowded with books, dragon figurines, seashells, crystals, and jeweled photographs of friends and family. Gwen had to grin. The clutter of curios and fantasy was like her own room back home.

"Finn? I mean, Findabhair?" she called. "It's me. Gwen. I'm here."

At first there was no response from the humped shape in the bed. Then came a grumble followed by a groan. Suddenly the duvet flew into the air.

"What's this?" cried Findabhair. "What am I doing here? I'm supposed to be at the airport meeting you!"

They screeched and hugged and laughed, talking at the same time, exclaiming over each other's appearance.

Three years had passed since they were last together, and both were now sixteen.

"Your dad said he gave up calling. I've unpacked and everything."

Findabhair looked ashamed for almost a second, then hurried to get dressed.

Though they were first cousins there was little resemblance between them, except for the golden-brown color of their hair. While Findabhair was tall and slender with a long mane that flowed over her shoulders, Gwen was short and plump with a head of cropped curls.

"You look amazing," Gwen said enviously. She flung herself on the bed. "And here's me. Blimp City."

Findabhair frowned as she pulled on black jeans, black T-shirt, and heavy black boots.

"Everyone in America wants to be skinny, don't they? It's daft. You shouldn't knock yourself so much. You look brilliant."

"Thanks." Gwen grinned at her cousin's clothes. "Do you work in a funeral home or what?"

Findabhair surveyed the loud pink shirt Gwen was wearing over denims and running shoes. "Does that top come with a battery?"

"I promised my mom we wouldn't fight."

"Me too."

They snickered.

It was easy to slip into their old banter. Despite living on opposite sides of the Atlantic, they had been best friends since they could walk and talk. As well as holidays spent together, they did their best to stay in touch through letters and e-mails.

"Don't you just love *The Return of the King*?" said Gwen. "I watch it constantly."

She was rummaging through her cousin's books, CDs, and DVDs. So many were identical to her own.

"To die for!" Findabhair agreed. She sat at her dressing table and put on her makeup. "I can't believe I'm in love with a man over forty. When he sang at the end, I nearly swooned. My king, my king."

"I thought you preferred Legolas?"

"I did at first. The elves are fabulous, so like my idea of the fairy folk. But doesn't he seem kind of sexless to you?"

Gwen didn't answer. There were many ways she was *not* like her cousin.

"I brought you an album of the Dropkick Murphys," she said instead. "I think you'll like them, especially their cover of 'The Rocky Road to Dublin.'"

"Great name, shame about the music. You know I *hate* folk."

"It's not. They're Irish-American punk-trad-grunge."

Gwen moved to the window to gaze out at the Irish Sea. She loved this old house in Bray that overlooked the seafront, sheltered by the Wicklow Mountains. Below her was the garden with its lilac and apple trees, enclosed by a stone wall. Past the wall was the road and a stretch of green lawn that lay before the promenade and the beach.

Some things had changed since her last visit. The old-style lampposts were gone, replaced with wooden fixtures like the masts of tall sailing ships. The wrought-iron railings had been painted dark-blue. Beyond the promenade was the seashore, with a spread of gray-blue stones, patches of wet sand, and tangles of seaweed like knotted hair. The sea itself shone in the sunlight, with summery waves charging to the strand like white horses. So many childhood memories belonged to this place. So many secret hopes and dreams.

"Right, I'm human," Findabhair declared.

She admired herself in the mirror, pleased with the contrast of black kohl and pale powder.

Gwen looked worried.

"Have you changed utterly?" she blurted out.

"What do you mean?"

"Are you crazy about boys, shopping, makeup?"

Findabhair nodded. "Yes, to all of the above."

Gwen's heart sank. Then she caught the mischief in her cousin's eyes, followed by a wicked grin.

"Don't panic, I haven't gone shallow altogether. I still seek the Faraway Country."

Findabhair spoke the last sentence grandly. It was a password between them, referring to their love of fantasy in every form—books, music, movies, art. Even the last time they had met, though both were almost thirteen, they had resumed their search for a door or passageway that might lead to other worlds.

The two stared at each other now without speaking. Gwen's silhouette glowed in the window, haloed by the light behind her. Findabhair was a double image, reflected in her looking glass like a shadowy Alice.

"Isn't that why you're here?" Findabhair said. "Aren't we heading off on a magical mystery tour?"

Gwen felt as if she might burst with happiness. Despite outward appearances, it seemed nothing had really changed. She had been so careful in her correspondence, afraid that Findabhair would think her childish. They had talked about traveling and various places to visit, but never about the true heart of their journey. Yet here, all along, her cousin had taken for granted what Gwen had been nursing as a secret dream.

Findabhair spread a map of Ireland over the floor.

"Listen, we've got to get our story down pat. I've promised the parents we're taking bus tours all the way and staying in *An Óige* youth hostels. But no way are we doing this. We haven't the hope of an adventure if we stick to the straight and narrow. We've got to go the road less traveled."

Gwen did her best to hide her anxiety. She was not at all happy about lying to her aunt and uncle. She was also wondering just how far from the path they would have to go. The map of the Thirty-Two Counties shimmered before her like the green-and-gold flag of an enchanted land. A thrill ran through her. What her cousin said was true. If they played it safe, how could they possibly find what they were looking for?

"Our first stop is Tara," Findabhair announced. "Loads of buses go there. Da will be happy to put us on one. After that, we can thumb our way around."

Gwen was dumbfounded. "I thought we were going to start at Newgrange? Didn't we agree to leave Tara till the end? Save the best for the last?"

"I know what's best, I'm the one who lives here," her cousin stated. "All roads lead to Tara, the royal center of Ireland. The sooner we get there, the better."

"I can't believe you're doing this!" Gwen spluttered. "It's not fair. The trip belongs to both of us. You're not the boss of it!"

A major fight seemed inevitable, with every possibility that the journey might end before it began. Though Gwen rarely stood up to her strong-willed cousin, she could stand her ground when pushed too far.

Suddenly confused and uncertain, Findabhair relented. Something nagged at the back of her mind, something she needed to tell Gwen if only she could remember. Her cousin was right. It *was* unfair to change their plans and insist on her own way. And yet . . .

She rubbed her forehead.

"Sorry," she conceded at last. "I'm being Ms. Bossy-Boots. Fine, then, no need to come to blows. We'll leave Tara to the last. But we're not doing the tourist trail. Agreed?"

"Agreed," said Gwen with relief.

They bent over the map once more.

"Newgrange it is," Findabhair said, tapping the ancient site on the River Boyne. "The *Brugh na Bóinne*."

"The fairy palace of Aengus Óg," Gwen said dreamily.

"The young god of love," her cousin sighed.

They both giggled.

"We're hopeless romantics," said Findabhair.

"Hope*ful*," Gwen corrected her.

Two

The summer sun warmed the gray highway that traversed the Plain of Meath. Gwen pressed her face to the bus window as the countryside flew past her like wings. Despite the occasional spire of a town or village, the land had risen to claim its ascendancy. This was the Ireland she dreamed of: silence falling over sage-green fields, hedgerows scarved with mist, clouds rising behind the hills like pale hills themselves.

Beside her, Findabhair was less enchanted with the journey. On a coach filled with tourists from America, Japan, Germany, and France, they were the youngest passengers.

"By decades, if not centuries," Findabhair had muttered when they climbed aboard. "We've joined the Blue Rinse Brigade."

Their fellow travelers were chiefly pensioners laden down with food parcels, cameras, maps, money belts, and guidebooks. Most wore big woolen sweaters to ward off the damp Irish air.

"They're very nice," Gwen had countered, delighted with the amount of sweets and treats that kept coming her way. "We're on a granny bus!"

Unlike her cousin, she was also enjoying the singalong orchestrated by the driver with the help of his microphone.

A gypsy rover came o'er the hill,
And down to the valley so shady,
He whistled and he sang,
Till the green woods rang,
And he won the heart of a la-a-a-dy.

"I *hate* folk music," Findabhair groaned.

She snorted impatiently as Gwen inspected yet another box of chocolates offered over the seat in front of them.

Then the bus swerved.

The movement was so violent, the chocolates flew into the air.

"Hey!"

Gwen scrambled to retrieve what she could, but most went rolling down the aisle.

The bus swerved again. Some of the passengers cried out in alarm. The microphone was still on, and they could hear the driver swearing.

Findabhair climbed over Gwen to look out the window.

"We're being rammed!" she yelled, excited.

Though she couldn't see clearly, a car appeared to be cramming their lane and sideswiping the coach.

They swerved again.

Gwen choked back her fear. There were no seat belts. What if they crashed? *I'm too young to die.* Why didn't the driver slow down! Was he trying to kill them? She fought the urge to cling onto Findabhair. Her cousin didn't look frightened. In fact, she looked exhilarated.

Now the bus careened off the road and into a field. Everyone was screaming. A series of bumps followed as they hit rough ground. Luggage spilled from the over-head racks. People ducked to avoid being struck by flying objects. Gwen gripped the armrests till her knuckles went white. Would the bus topple over? She was sick with terror.

At last, the coach jerked to a halt in the middle of the field.

Silence.

Followed by a burst of glossolalic babble as everyone began talking at once in their various languages. Some wept quietly.

"Order, please, order," the driver called out. He stood in the aisle, white-faced and shaken. "Is everyone all right? Anyone injured? Help is on the way. I've put in a call. Could everyone please stay calm."

"Come on, let's get out of here," Findabhair said to Gwen.

She had retrieved their knapsacks and sleeping bags from the floor. Face flushed, eyes bright, she dragged Gwen behind her.

"Shouldn't we wait for the police?"

"Are you mad? We'll be stuck here all day. This is our chance to scarper. We've got places to go, things to do."

Gwen didn't resist. The other passengers were disembarking too. Everyone wanted to feel firm ground underfoot. No one was badly hurt but all were in shock, and they huddled together in little groups to comfort one another.

Standing alone in the meadow, the bus looked like a big lumbering animal that had lost its way. Beyond it, the highway rolled on into the distance. Cars and trucks sped past, oblivious to their plight. They were caught between two towns, in the middle of nowhere.

Ignoring Gwen's protests, Findabhair walked determinedly to the edge of the road and stuck out her thumb.

"Don't worry, it's broad daylight. We won't get in if anyone looks like an ax murderer."

"Like we could tell!"

Gwen was about to say more when they both spotted the battered little car heading their way. It was already slowing down as it approached them.

"What a dote!" cried Findabhair.

Though it had seen better days, the Triumph Herald retained a dignity of its own. The rounded body and humped roof gave it a homely, friendly look. The rusted chrome on the headlights looked like bushy eyebrows. The forest-green paint was mottled and chipped like a freckled face.

When the car drew up beside them, they peered inside to scrutinize the driver.

He suited his vehicle. A wizened little man, he had a face like a dried apple and two bright beads for eyes. His suit was worn and frayed, of green tweed with brown stitching, and the jacket was closed with a big safety pin. On his head was a peaked cap, the same ruddy red color as his cheeks.

He leaned over to open the passenger door. Without hesitation Findabhair got in, and unlocked the rear door for her cousin. Gwen had no choice but to follow or be left behind. Furious, she climbed in the back.

"Now, where may I take you, my fine ladies?" asked the little man, craning his neck to look at Gwen, then squinting at Findabhair as she banged the door shut.

"We're off to Newgrange," Findabhair said airily, "to give our regards to Aengus Óg."

The interior of the car was as dilapidated as its owner. Threadbare blankets covered rips in the upholstery. The teak dashboard was pockmarked with woodworm. Scattered over the floor and the backseat were heaps of old shoes and boots. Findabhair noted the moss on the carpet at her feet, and the pink bells of foxglove sprouting from the ashtray. She turned around to grin at Gwen. *Isn't this hilarious?*

Gwen glared back.

"Sure what would ye want with the *Brugh na Bóinne*," the old man was saying. "There's nothing there but for-

eigners. Wouldn't ye druther go to *Teamhair na Ríogh*? If
it's leprechauns and pots of gold ye want, Tara's your
only man."

His voice had a wheedling tone that made Gwen
uneasy, but Findabhair was enjoying his eccentricity.

"What do we look like, a pair of gobs?" she retorted.
"We don't believe in leprechauns with pots of gold."

"Then ye wouldn't put any faith in the likes of the
Good People?"

His persistence reached a higher note. In the back,
Gwen heard a warning in that quaver, but Findabhair
continued indignantly.

"If you mean wee things with wings and shoemakers
with pointy ears—*no*. That's a load of commercial rub-
bish exploiting the true heart of the legends."

As Findabhair warmed to her subject, exhorting on
the abuses of Irish mythology, Gwen eyed the plethora of
footwear around her. Buckled shoes and ladies' slippers,
high heels and working boots, some with worn-out soles
and holes in the toes, others with tongues hanging out
and their laces missing. Not one had a visible match. She
found herself wondering about the shape of the little
man's ears hidden by his cap. Without thinking, she
leaned forward to interrupt her cousin.

"We do believe in something. The something that's
in the ancient tales and poetry. That's why we're traveling. It's sort of a quest. To see if that something still
exists."

A silence settled inside the car. Gwen's words seemed to hang in the air, glittering with meaning, as if they were more important than she had intended them to be. She felt suddenly nervous.

"Ah now." The old man's cackle broke the tension. "You've left me behind with your fanciful blather."

He stopped the car.

"Out ye go, the pair of ye."

His dismissal was curt. They sat stunned for a minute. Then they spotted the signpost on the road in front of them.

TEAMHAIR. TARA.

"What?" Findabhair exclaimed.

"H-h-how?" Gwen stammered.

Caught up in the old man's talk, neither had paid any attention to the route they were taking.

"Up that boreen ye go, and what you're looking for will find ye."

"Ta for the lift," said Findabhair, disoriented.

"Have a nice day," Gwen added automatically.

They were still standing, stupefied, when the little car drove off.

Findabhair shrugged. "I guess we're starting here after all."

They heaved their knapsacks onto their backs and walked down the lane that led to Tara. The way was lined with tall hawthorn trees laden with white blossoms like brides. Bees hummed in the dense greenery. Branches met overhead to form an arched roof, like a leafy hall leading to a throne room.

"Did he give you the creeps?" Gwen asked her cousin.

They stepped into the verge to let a tour bus crawl past.

"What? Not at'all. He was good crack, odd as two left feet. I just don't like all that shamrocks-and-leprechauns lark. He was treating us like tourists."

"I don't think so," Gwen said, troubled. "He was testing us somehow, trying to find out something. And I think he succeeded. I should have kept my big yap shut."

"I'm sure he hadn't a bog's notion what you were on about. Daft as a brush."

Gwen was not reassured. In fact, she suspected the opposite was true. Though she couldn't explain how or why, she felt that the little man understood her words even more than she did. The disquieting feeling would have continued to nag at her if Tara itself hadn't presented a distraction.

THREE

Y ahoo!" said Gwen. "A restaurant! I'm starving!"
The road had brought them to a souvenir shop
and tea room. The smell of baked goods wafted through
the air. The sounds of cutlery and conversation echoed
from the lace-curtained windows. There were also
tables and chairs outside, in a tidy garden with rose-
bushes and trimmed hedges. To the right was a parking
lot and further beyond, the iron gates that led to the
Hill of Tara.

"You told me to keep you from stuffing yourself,"
Findabhair reminded her.

"I meant soda bread and sausages, and fattening
things like that. Something small will do. All this excitement makes me want to eat."

"First Tara, then food."

"Bossy-boots," muttered Gwen.

To the unknowing eye, Tara was no more than a ram-
bling expanse of windy hilltop. Its name meant simply "a
place from which there is a wide prospect." Indeed, to the

unknowing eye, Tara held no other charm than the magnificent view of the surrounding countryside. In all directions, the fertile lands of the central plain of Meath stretched to distant borders of misty mountains and the blue rim of the sea.

For Gwen and Findabhair, there was so much more. This royal residence and center had been the pulse of Ireland for over two thousand years. *Bright-surfaced Teamhair*, the poets called her. Tara of Kings. The glory of the place was subtle and secret. It lingered in the shadows of the tall grasses that covered the mounds and earthworks. It whispered on the wind. *Cnoc na mBan-Laoch*. The Hill of the Women-Heroes. On this green knoll assembled the female warriors, golden torcs at their throats, slender spears in their hands. Not until the seventh century A.D. and the Christian laws of *Cáin Adamnáin* were women banned from warfare. *Teach Míodchuarta*. The Banquet Hall. A long sunken trench between two parallel banks, it was once a house of noble proportions. Fourteen doors graced its high walls: seven to face the golden sun, seven to face the silver moon. *Ráth na Ríogh*. The Royal Enclosure. In ages past, this broad circle housed a kingly fort crowned with a palisade of oak. Here was held the great *Feis* of Tara, the coronation ritual in which the King wed the Goddess of the land.

The girls left their knapsacks at the gate to roam freely over fosse and ridge. In a happy daze, they told themselves that they were treading in the footsteps of kings and queens, Druids and warriors. They imagined the gatherings for games and festivals, the making of laws, and the hosting of armies. They shivered at the thought of lunar feasts that saw mysterious rites and ritual sacrifices.

Gwen climbed onto the Grave Mound of the Hostages, a small green hill like an upturned bowl. A strange lassitude came over her. She lay down in the grass, which was warm from the sun. Overhead, the clouds moved across the blue plain of the sky. They were traveling swiftly, herded like sheep by the wind. At the corner of her eye, a black beetle scuttled over the ground. Nearby a snail clung to a green stalk, fast asleep, its shell a spiral of cream and brown. Gwen felt lost and glad, caught up in the flow of forever.

Ever restless and active, Findabhair was searching the site like a hunter's hound. Arriving at the mound from a different angle, she discovered the opening in the hill. It was barred by a metal gate with a padlock.

"It's a cairn!" she called up to Gwen, who didn't answer.

Findabhair pressed her face to the railings and peered into the dimness. Just as she had thought. Despite its appearance as a grassy hill, the mound was man-made with heavy slabs of stone. The interior was dark and hollow, like a cave. Or a tomb. She shivered. There were carvings on the great stone to her left. She could barely make out the circular designs, spiraling eyes and snakes swallowing their tails. She wished she knew what they meant. A yearning came over her. She wanted to get inside.

On top of the mound, Gwen had lapsed into a daydream. The clouds were falling out of the sky, descending upon her. The crest of the hill was a green island in a misty lake. Her ears began to throb with a low thrumming sound. Her blood thrilled in response, the way feet itch to dance. Under the hum—or was it beyond?—came the trace of music. It seemed to come from a great depth or distance, like the sigh of a conch. There was a rumbling like far-off drums or thunder, but also high reedy notes like a flute or a lark. She strained to listen but the throbbing interfered, as if her ears were not attuned to such sounds.

Below her, Findabhair leaned against the gate, eyes half-closed. She too was wrapped in a milky stillness, listening to the unearthly music. Then another sound reached her. The fierce gallop of a horse. As the hooves drew near, a voice called out through the mist.

Come to the Sídhe-mound under the hill.

On the hilltop, Gwen was suddenly awake. Storm clouds had moved across the sun like the dark swirl of a cape. The grass felt cold and damp at her back. She scrambled to her feet.

"Where are you?" she cried.

Findabhair jumped away from the gate as if it had burned her. Bewildered, she looked up at Gwen who stared wildly down.

Without a word they ran from the grave mound. Grabbing their knapsacks, they dashed to the tea room as if pursued by the hounds of hell. Only when they were safely inside, surrounded by people, did they meet each other's eyes. With cups of tea and buttered scones in front of them, they could acknowledge the truth.

"It's here," Gwen whispered.

"It still exists." Findabhair nodded.

Barely able to breathe, they grinned at each other.

"I feel like standing on the table and roaring it out at the top of my lungs."

Findabhair had lowered her voice so she wouldn't give in to the temptation.

"I know what you mean. I could run up a mountain or leap off a cliff!"

Gwen slurped her tea loudly. They burst into a fit of giggles. Both felt light-headed and giddy.

"Can you remember what happened?"

Findabhair frowned with the effort, but it was too like a dream. The kind that hinted with vague images but couldn't be recalled. She shook her head.

"Me neither," Gwen sighed. "It's gone. But there was something . . . like . . . an invitation?"

"Yes! Exactly! So how do we accept?"

Gwen was attacked by misgivings.

"Should we? Weren't you afraid?"

"Definitely! The unknown would scare the bejaysus out of anyone. But you wouldn't let that stop you, would you?"

"I suppose not," Gwen hedged.

She wasn't as headstrong as her cousin, but she didn't want to be left behind, either.

"We'll camp overnight in the mound," declared Findabhair.

"Omigod!" wailed Gwen.

The couple at the next table glanced over at them. Findabhair continued inexorably.

"I've always wanted to sleep in a mound or on top of a rath. You know that's the best way to enter Faerie. It's in all the old tales and the *aislings*, the vision-poems."

She closed her eyes a moment as a thought flitted through her mind. Something to do with a *Sídhe*-mound, and Tara as well. Something in a book? The memory teased her, but remained elusive. Nevertheless she had made her decision. But would her cousin agree?

Despite the self-confessed yellow stripe down her back, Gwen was seriously considering the proposition. By no coincidence was she facing this dilemma. Hadn't she traveled to Ireland in search of adventure? It *was* the kind of risk that suited a quest. Though a hundred doubts and fears assailed her, some queenly part inside was giving the royal nod.

"You realize we'll be breaking the law," she pointed out. "Trespassing and who knows what else."

"Forced entry. There's a padlock on the gate." Findabhair was jubilant. If her cousin was working on the details, she was obviously in for the count. "If we get nicked, you do the talking. When they hear the American accent, they'll go easy on us."

"Never mind the accent," Gwen said, swallowing her fear. "We won't get caught."

Four

It was almost midnight when they returned to Tara. They had spent the day in the village of Dunshaughlin, window-shopping, strolling around, and dawdling over fish and chips in the local diner. For safety and secrecy, they chose to walk the long road back.

As they trudged through the dim landscape, Gwen kept an eye on the passing traffic. She found herself thinking about the odd little man.

"Do you really not believe in leprechauns and 'wee things with wings'?" she asked her cousin.

"You mean fairies at the bottom of the garden?" Findabhair snorted. "You must be joking. That's not what I'm looking for."

Gwen's tone was wistful. "I loved those little flower fairies when I was a kid. Still do."

"You're a sad human being."

When they arrived at Tara, it was dark and empty. The tea room was closed with its windows shuttered. The tables and chairs had been taken inside. The girls hurried furtively across the parking lot, and scrambled over the stone wall onto the hill.

In the silence of the night, Tara was a desolate place. The shadowy earthworks were like graves rising up from the grasses. The humped shapes of the mounds seemed ready to pounce. Nervously, the two kept looking around. They knew they were treading on forbidden ground. A chill wind raised goose bumps over their skin. They couldn't shake the sense that they were being watched.

"Hold the torch steady," Findabhair hissed.

They were crouched in front of the Grave Mound of the Hostages. It loomed ominously over them.

Gwen trained the flashlight on the gate that barred their way. She was still battling with second thoughts. But there was no turning back. *You've put your toe in the water, might as well get wet.*

Gently, Findabhair worked the padlock with her penknife. For a while the only sound to be heard was the quick rasp of their breaths and the scraping of the knife. Then came a triumphant click.

"We're in."

They were too excited for last-minute doubts, too busy making themselves comfortable in the cramped inner space. It was like a small cave, cold and dank. They had to crawl to move about, spreading out their ground sheet and unrolling their sleeping bags. The walls and roof seemed to press in on them; the massive stones corbeled together and weighed down with sods of earth.

Findabhair played her flashlight over the biggest stone on the left. Circular designs whirled across the rock.

"They're like spiral galaxies," Gwen said, awed.

"We should lie with our heads against them," her cousin suggested.

"That's what the Druids did," Gwen agreed. *"In the heavy chambers of darkness."* Then she added uneasily, "I think we should stay dressed."

"For a quick escape?"

"You never know."

The flashlight lit up the cave like a little campfire, casting shadows around them. Once they were settled inside their sleeping bags, they turned it off. The darkness engulfed them. Neither could speak at first, overwhelmed by what they had done. The clammy scent of moldering earth was unmistakable. They were trapped in a tomb.

Slowly their eyes grew accustomed to the dimness, and they breathed more easily.

"What do you think might happen?" Gwen whispered.

"Anything. Nothing." Findabhair was serious. "I'm not sure I really care. Just to do this is an adventure in itself."

"I know what you mean. I wouldn't have done it on my own in a million years, but I love it. I'm really glad we're here."

"Me too." Findabhair let out a low laugh. "Anyone else would think we were mad."

"Guess what?" said Gwen. "I meant to tell you earlier. I was looking at the guidebook to Tara when you were in the restroom. There's a place nearby called Tobar Finn. What do you make of that?"

Findabhair was delighted.

"*Tobar* is the Irish word for 'well.' What a brilliant coincidence that it's named after me. I knew it was my destiny to come here!"

"Mine too. My name is the same as yours. Findabhair and Gwenhyvar. I've got the Welsh and you've got the Irish, but they both mean the same thing."

"Yes," her cousin murmured.

With a start, Findabhair turned on the flashlight and rummaged in her knapsack.

"What's up?" said Gwen.

"I can't believe I forgot to show you this! I've been carrying it around with me everywhere. I guess all the fuss of the trip put it out of my head. Have a look."

Gwen turned sideways in her sleeping bag to admire the little book bound in green with gold letters.

"*The Wyrd of the White Lady*," she said softly. The words echoed from the stones around them. "*Wyrd* means 'fate' in Old English, doesn't it? I love the title. We're both white ladies, really."

She turned the pages and began to read aloud.

Be fleet of foot, O fair Hunted One,
From the dark of the shadow—

"Stop!" Findabhair said suddenly. She was overcome with foreboding. "What made you pick that one?"

Gwen caught the panic in her cousin's voice and felt a tremor of the same fear.

"What's wrong?"

"I . . . I don't know."

Findabhair grabbed the book and shoved it back into her knapsack.

"Gwen, was I the only one who wanted to come to Tara? Were you against it?"

"Don't be silly. It was always on the agenda. I was dying to come. But later, not sooner."

"Then it could be me, or it could be you, or it could be both of us."

"Are you going to let me in on this train of thought or do I have to buy a ticket?"

Findabhair grinned sheepishly. "Sorry. I'll let you know as soon as I do. I think I had a dream about that book and now I'm getting premonitions."

"This is not the time and place! You're spooking me out! Let's leave it till the morning, okay?"

"You're right," Findabhair laughed. "What are we like? A pair of eejits!"

She turned off the flashlight. They continued to talk in low tones, about their school year, their interests, their friends and teachers, anything that didn't involve the quest. Though neither said it, each was haunted by a nameless dread. But eventually their conversation was punctuated by yawns, till they both dropped off to sleep.

Neither sensed the changes outside the mound. As darkness met light in the dim borderland before dawn, the stillness over Tara began to shudder. To come alive. Before time could cross from night to day, one world was about to eclipse another.

The abandoned earthworks began to glow as if a falling star had landed upon them. From the empty trench of the Banquet Hall rose the shining silhouette of a glorious palace. Walls of gold and silver glittered with gems. A thousand candles blazed within. From the graceful arch of high windows, sweet sounds issued forth: unearthly music, murmur, and laughter.

Padded footfalls came out of the shadows.

"There are humans in the mound!"

The whispers rustled in the wind.

"Does the King know of this?"

A wild laugh trilled like a panpipe.

"Have you not heard? Before this night is through, he will take them hostage!"

At that very moment Gwen turned in her sleep, troubled by a hint of warning. Beside her, Findabhair did the same. Their heads rested against the great stone behind them. As light seeped into the grooves of the spiral designs, they were both illumined by halos.

A voice called inside the mound.

"Gwenhyvar, fair one, Gwenhyvar fair!"

Gwen frowned in her sleep. Behind her eyelids motes of light joined together to form an image at the foot of her sleeping bag. He was a youth of her own age, slender and naked. His skin shone palely in the dark. Around his neck were beads of jet and amber.

"You must leave this place! Be fleet of foot!"

Though she was dreaming, Gwen sensed that the danger was real. She wrestled against the bonds of sleep, but her efforts sent her tumbling dizzily through space and colors.

"Help me!" she cried to the boy.

"I cannot," he said sadly, as he faded away. "I am only a barrow wight. A shadow of my self long gone. I died in this place many centuries ago. I have no power other than to warn you. For I, too, was a hostage. I, too, was the Hunted and the Sacrificed."

His words made her blood run cold. What terrible thing had happened to hold his spirit to this mound? What terrible thing might happen again?

Even as Gwen struggled to wake, Findabhair was dancing her way through a seductive fantasy. She was at a fancy-dress ball. Everyone wore gorgeous costumes of silk and satin, with sparkling masks and peacock plumes. She herself was dressed in a gown of shimmering midnight with a black feathered cloak. Her hair was caught up in a crespine of pearls. Swirling and twirling at a breathtaking pace, she waltzed in the arms of a startling young man. As is the way of dreams, he was somehow familiar though she didn't know him. His features were hawklike, his eyes dark and piercing. His raven-black hair fell to his shoulders. Upon his forehead glittered a star. He didn't appear to be speaking, but words spun in her mind in time to the music.

O Lady, if thou comest to my proud people,
'Tis a golden crown shall circle thy head,
Thou shalt dwell by the sweet streams of
   my country,
And drink mead and wine in the arms of
   thy lover.

His arm tightened around her waist.

"Come with me."

It was more a command than a request.

There was no beginning to the dream, so Findabhair didn't consider an end. In that moment there was only the music and the dance and the dark eyes of her suitor.

Yes.

The word sighed on her lips as she lay sleeping. Beside her Gwen turned again, sensing the doom that was upon them.

The clatter of hooves. A wild charge in the night. Louder and louder as the horse drew near. The gate of the mound burst open! The inner core was now immense, a stone cathedral. In galloped a stallion, darker than the shadows, nostrils flared and snorting flame. Astride the horse was a black-caped rider with a face as sharp as a hawk's.

He swooped for his prey.

"No!" cried Gwen.

The horse reared up. The rider glared down. There was no remorse or pity in those sloe-black eyes.

"'No' is your answer but 'yes' was hers. I take my bride from the Mound of the Hostages!"

Plucking Findabhair from the ground, sleeping bag and all, he slung her over his saddle.

Then he rode from the mound.

"No!" screeched Gwen once more, loud enough to wake herself at last.

Weak and trembling, she reached for her cousin to seek comfort from the nightmare. New terror gorged her throat.

Findabhair was gone.

Five

Gwen couldn't believe what her eyes were telling her. Findabhair and everything belonging to her had vanished! There had to be a simple explanation. Her cousin had woken early and gone for a walk. Or maybe she was playing a joke on Gwen. That would be just like her. She was probably in the tea room right now, ordering their breakfast.

Gwen pulled on her shoes and scrambled out of the mound.

It was a damp drizzly morning. The sky was gray and cloudy. Trails of mist snaked through the grasses. As if to outrun her fears, Gwen raced from the hill and across the parking lot. The tea room was closed. Her heart sank. The windows were still shuttered like lidded eyes. Back to the hill she ran, over the earthworks, calling out Findabhair's name. Her cries echoed on the air like a lonesome wind.

No response.

No Findabhair.

At last she stood still as the truth struck home. Her cousin was gone. She had been abducted. But by whom? Or *what*?

Gwen fought back the tears. Slowly she recalled the night's dreams and visitations, confirming a reality she could barely accept. It was all very well to set out on a quest to seek things unimaginable, fantastical, and unknown. It was quite a different matter to find them. Only now did she admit that she hadn't really believed in that other world. It had all been in the realm of the imagination. Till now.

"She's been stolen by the fairies."

The words issued from Gwen's mouth on the mist of her breath, shivering in the air.

"What am I going to do?" she wailed.

Dazed, she wandered around the site like a lost soul, reluctant to leave the place where she had last seen her cousin. Returning to the Grave Mound of the Hostages, she packed up her things. As she replaced the padlock on the gate, the click of finality made her wince. Findabhair would not be found here again. The rider had taken her away. But to where?

Unable to stem the tears any longer, she wept openly as she trudged down the road. What should she do? What *could* she do? Call her aunt and uncle? Contact the police? A kidnapping had occurred. Words from her dream came back to haunt her. *I, too, was a hostage. I, too, was the Hunted and the Sacrificed.* A wave of panic washed over her. She had to do something! And quick!

There was no question of going back to her aunt and uncle. What could she tell them? Nor was there anyone she could ask for help. Who would believe her? There was only one option. She would have to rescue Findabhair herself.

Despite the panic this decision engendered in Gwen, she began to feel a little better. She also began to think. The fairies were the enemy. What did she know about them? Behind the tales told to modern children was an old peasant belief in another race who lived alongside humans. They were called "the Good People," not because they were good, but because they needed to be appeased. *For when they were good, they were very very good, but when they were bad, they were horrid.* Some legends claimed they were gods. Others said they were fallen angels; not good enough for heaven but not bad enough for hell. Descriptions varied in all the books and stories. They could be tiny and winged like butterflies, or taller than trees in fiery columns of light and shadow. Though they didn't dislike humans, they often played tricks on them, sometimes cruel ones. Their favorite mortals were little children, beautiful youths, and generous adults.

Like the Irish weather, their temperament was unpredictable and ever-changeable, moving swiftly from storms of passion to sunny humors. They were willful and capricious and wild as the wind, loved music, dancing, and perpetual frolic. Their palaces were found under hills, in deep forests, and dark mountain caves. They also dwelt in coral castles beneath the sea. They might be glimpsed scurrying in an eddy of green leaves, or dancing at night in moonlit woods. Their voices could be heard in the plash of waves or faint echoes on the wind. The bending swathe of barley across the fields marked the path of the Elfin King and his Court.

The more she thought about it, the more disheartened Gwen grew. What did any of this mean? How could she use it? She was missing Findabhair in more ways than one. While Gwen was the steadier of the two, with more common sense, Findabhair was the daring one who made all the decisions. She always knew what to do.

"It's not fair," Gwen groaned. "The game has started and I'm only half a team!"

When she reached the main road, she stopped in surprise. There in front of her, as if waiting patiently, was the battered Triumph Herald. It shone with a fresh coat of green paint, but inside sat the same wizened little man.

He beckoned to her.

After all that had happened, Gwen knew without a doubt what she had only suspected the day before. Flinging her knapsack into the car, she plumped down in the front seat to confront the leprechaun.

"Now don't be leppin' on me as if I'm to blame," he said quickly. "Fair's fair. Ye got what ye came for. I'm here to lend a hand."

With a crunch of gears, he moved the old car into traffic. Perched on two telephone books, white and yellow pages, he peered over the dashboard like a child at the wheel.

"I'll get ye to Busáras in plenty of time to break your fast. Your bus leaves at ten o'clock sharp."

"And where am I going, if that's not too much to ask?" Gwen said archly.

At the same time she was feeling a huge sense of relief. The cavalry had arrived. All was not lost. And behind her relief was the rising thrill of excitement. Was this an adventure or what!

As if he could read her mind, the leprechaun chuckled.

"Ye were looking for somethin' and now it's found ye. Make the most of it. The fairy court is on its summer circuit of the country. Ye'll have to be fleet-footed and quick-witted if ye want to find your kin."

"Is she all right?"

"Right in the head? Is that what ye mean?"

"Is she safe?" Gwen persisted, annoyed with his antics.

"That's a quare word. Is she safe and sound, are ye askin' me?"

His cackle was disturbing. Despite his small size, there was something sinister about him. He was like the ventriloquist dummies that always gave her the heebie-jeebies.

"Sound in the head and safe in her bed," he continued. "Have ye any right to demand that, after barging into secret places without so much as a by-your-leave? If it's safety and soundness ye wanted, ye'd have been better off follyin' the Yankee trail to Killarney and all that blarney. There's only one thing the fairy folk ask of your kind and that's to be left alone. Ye broke more laws than your own when ye slept in the mound."

Gwen shifted uncomfortably at his tirade. The leprechaun had gone red in the face, stealing the righteous indignation that had helped her be so bold.

"We didn't know," she said lamely.

"Ye did too," he retorted.

He was relentless. Gwen slumped in her seat. She knew Findabhair wouldn't have let him browbeat her into silence, but she wasn't Findabhair. With a sigh, she looked out the window. The countryside was speeding past in a multicolored blur. The car was going incredibly fast for something so old. As if it had wings.

"Okay. We did know what we were doing. Sort of. I guess we have to take the consequences. What happens next?"

"That's the spirit," said the little man, in a friendlier tone. "We all love a contest and ye are two fine girls, strong and true. We'll get great sport out of ye."

Gwen flinched. Hardly a comforting thought. And now an even less pleasant one struck her.

"Were you the one who drove our bus off the road?"

His wicked chuckle answered the question before he did.

"A tidy bit of manhooverin' that."

"You could have killed someone!"

"Well I didn't, did I? So give yourself a rest. The two of ye were way offtrack, like Wrong-Way Corrigan. I had to set ye's right agin."

He started to fiddle with the antique radio in the dashboard. Gwen was surprised that it worked and more surprised at what it played. The Dropkick Murphys' frenetic rendition of "The Rocky Road to Dublin" ricocheted off the windshield and around the car.

Then off to reap the corn,
Leave where I was born,
Cut a stout blackthorn
To banish ghosts and goblins.
A brand-new pair of brogues,
Rattlin' o'er the bogs,
Frightening all the dogs,
On the rocky road to Dublin.

"Aren't they the boyos?" said the leprechaun, bobbing his head to the music like a crazed noddy dog. "Asha, it's not much of a rocky road these days, is it? With all these fancy carriageways."

One-two-three-four-five
Hunt the hare and turn her
Down the rocky road
And all the way to Dublin
Whack fol lol dee dah.

They were indeed on the road to Dublin, as Gwen could see from the signs along the motorway. Pushing well over a hundred kilometers an hour, the little car kept pace with the speeding traffic. As they overtook a tractor-trailer hogging the right lane, the little man made a rude gesture at the driver.

"Them articulated lorries think they own the road."

The truck driver blasted his horn.

"Up the yard!" roared the leprechaun.

They approached the capital city through the spacious grounds of Phoenix Park. Deer grazed on the green lawns. Few strollers were about. As they passed Áras an Uachtaráin, the palatial home of the Irish President, the little man doffed his hat.

"Your store of happiness to ye, *Mná na hÉireann!*" he shouted in a fulsome tone.

Gwen caught a glimpse of his pointy ears before the cap was clapped back on.

"A grand lady she is, our Mary," he said. "She believes in us, ye know, as do all truehearts, not like the rest of them blackguard politicians."

The Triumph shot out of the park like a bullet and into the early morning bustle of Dublin City. Pedestrian lights seemed irrelevant to the leprechaun as he plowed through intersections, scattering the crowds.

"You'd make a good cabby in New York," Gwen commented, gripping her seat.

"Heh? What's that?"

But all his attention was on the road as he switched lanes with abandon. Swerving past a double-decker bus, they flew down the quays, the River Liffey a brown streak. They had just begun a death-defying race with an overloaded milk van, when the traffic on O'Connell Bridge brought them to a halt.

"We're early," the leprechaun muttered, glancing at the clock that hung over the Harp Lounge. "How about a jaunt round the oul town? Show you the sights? I'm an urban elf meself."

"I've done the Dublin Bus Tour," Gwen said quickly, hoping it would deter him.

It didn't. For the next twenty minutes, she endured the most bizarre sightseeing excursion imaginable. Dashing through the thousand-year-old city at break-neck speed, the leprechaun shouted out names of various attractions that Gwen knew couldn't be right.

As they headed up the broad thoroughfare of O'Connell Street, they passed a modern sculpture cum fountain. It depicted the River Liffey's goddess, Anna Livia, lounging in a narrow concrete trough.

"That's the Floozy-in-the-Jacuzzi!" roared the leprechaun.

Just beyond the fountain a new monument soared into the sky, the elegant metal needle called the Spire.

"Stiletto-in-the-Ghetto!"

After an illegal U-turn at Parnell's statue, they drove back across the Liffey, past the venerable Trinity College, and into Grafton's shopping street mall. The little man had begun to sing, completely out of key.

In Dublin's fair city,
Where the girls are so pretty,
I first set my eyes on Sweet Molly Malone.

"Tart-with-the-Cart!" he announced, as they passed the buxom brass of Molly Malone beside her wheelbarrow of cockles and mussels. "Alive, alive-oh!"

Gwen closed her eyes. Traffic was banned from this street, but they were weaving around the pedestrians.

"You've missed the Time-in-the-Slime," the leprechaun remarked, "the clock that was counting down to the new millennium. It was just under the water line at the bridge. Wonder where it went. Maybe it flew."

He chortled away at his own joke, and didn't seem to notice that he had long left his passenger behind, figuratively.

By the time they came to a stop, brakes screeching, in front of the Central Bus Station, Gwen was utterly bewitched, bothered, and bewildered.

"Here ye are now," he said. "Go west, young woman, to Galway Town. Make your way to the Burren in the County of Clare. There'll be a banquet tonight at twilight. Carron is the nearest human habitation. Use your wits and ye'll find it."

He hauled her knapsack out of the car and leaned it

against the glass doors of the station. Gwen didn't move. Though she couldn't say she liked the leprechaun, he was her only link to the fairies.

"Couldn't you drive me there?" she pleaded with him. "I'll pay for the gas, for your time."

"Sure what would I want with them bits of paper? Isn't it always becoming less with that deflation business?"

As he opened the door to hurry her out, his eyes suddenly narrowed with a greedy gleam.

"Have ye any gold on ye?"

"No," she said forlornly.

"Away ye go, then. I've done me job. I was to point ye in the general direction and that's what I've done. Good day to ye."

He got back behind the wheel and turned the key of the ignition. Desperate, Gwen ran to his window.

"Please," she begged.

The little man hesitated. Was that a hint of sympathy in his eyes? Or was it slyness? He cocked his head.

"Ye've me heart scalded with your moanin', but I'll say this for ye, you've got pluck. There wasn't a squeak out of ye about the drivin'. I'll give ye a word of wisdom. If you're betwixt and between, trust the one with red hair. Now that's more than I should be tellin' ye. I'm off. I've shoes to mend."

The Triumph Herald disappeared around the corner, along with her last hope of a direct route to Findabhair.

Dejected, Gwen picked up her knapsack and walked into the station.

After all she had been through, it was unsettling to be suddenly faced with the ordinary. People sat on benches waiting for their buses, reading newspapers, or talking on their cell phones. Ranged around the station were a cafeteria, pub, newsagent, and ticket office. She felt disoriented, straddling two worlds, unsure of what was real.

The door of the cafeteria opened and the rich smell of bacon tickled her nose. She read the sign hungrily. FULL IRISH BREAKFAST.   5.00 RASHERS, EGG, BLACK AND WHITE PUDDING, GRILLED TOMATOES, FRIED POTATOES, MUSHROOMS, AND BEANS. SERVED WITH BUTTERED TOAST AND A POT OF TEA.

If she ate that, she'd be ready for anything! She checked the bus schedule. Plenty of time to eat, as the leprechaun had promised.

The waiter was a tall young man with red hair shaved on both sides of his head. His ears, nose, and eyebrow were pierced with tiny silver rings.

"The full monty?" he asked her.

"What?"

"D'ya want a big feed? Blood puddin' and all? Gowan, be a divil."

"Okay," she said, laughing, "I'll have a bit of everything."

Six

The bus left Dublin City behind and sped down the road on its way across Ireland. Gwen gazed out the window, alone and anxious. Was she waving or drowning? She kept alternating between a wild optimism that she could handle the situation and a despairing panic that she was in over her head. Mostly she was worried about Findabhair. The leprechaun had refused to say if her cousin was all right. What if she wasn't? Though Gwen tried hard not to, she couldn't help but dwell on the dark side of Faerie. A lot of the Grimms' stories were truly grim. What about the mermaid who danced on knives at the wedding? And all those kids eaten by witches and giants? Fairy tales did not always end "happily ever after." Nor did many of the modern fantasies she liked to read. Why on earth did she ever want to go on a quest? What could she have been thinking!

While her mind raced in frantic circles, her eyes rested on the country outside. Slowly but surely, Ireland worked its magic. A sudden rain showered the landscape.

The faraway hills were veiled in gray. Then the down-pour ceased as abruptly as it had started, leaving every-thing breathless and silvered. Hedgerows dripped sparkles of water. Puddles glistened at the side of the road. Now a splendid rainbow spanned the sky. Gwen was lulled by the beauty into a state of quiet bliss.

Though the bus traveled through towns and urban centers, the dreamy feeling stayed with her. The sight of bungalows, supermarkets, and gas stations only confirmed a notion that was growing inside her. There were two Irelands beyond her window, like layers of story on a palimpsest. One was a modern nation outfitted in technol-ogy, concrete, and industry. The other was a timeless pagan place that hinted continually of its presence. An old castle stood wedged into a terrace of new houses, a cloaked stranger in the crowd. High on a hilltop, above a factory, was a grove of sacred oak. A tractor plowed a field in the shadow of a stone circle. Behind the flashy hotel leaned a ruinous tower. Like a magician playing with colored scarves, the hidden land revealed itself in bright flashes and glimpses.

"It hasn't died," she murmured to herself, "only gone underground."

When the bus arrived in Galway City in the early afternoon, Gwen's distress returned full-blown. She hur-ried nervously through unknown streets. There were no familiar faces in the crowds that pressed against her. Eyre Square was thronged with young people lounging on the grass, shoppers taking a break, and workers eating their lunch in the sunshine. Vainly she hoped to spot someone she knew. *Findabhair, where are you?*

Her stomach grumbled at the vinegary smells from a fish-and-chip shop, but there was no time to eat. She needed to find the place the leprechaun had mentioned. His instructions were her only guide. *Make your way to the Burren in the County of Clare. There'll be a banquet tonight at twilight. Carron is the nearest human habitation.*

A bus brought her to the outskirts of Galway where she found a spot to hitchhike. She didn't like thumbing alone, but she had no choice. She was too unsure of where she was going to take public transportation. County Clare was south of Galway, according to her map, and that was all she knew.

When the sleek silver Mercedes drew up, Gwen looked inside. The car's interior was immaculate, pale-blue leather with dark-blue carpets. *Céilidh* music echoed from the radio. She studied the driver to assess his character. He was a businessman in a smart suit and tie. His briefcase lay on the floor beside him. Forty-something and slightly paunchy, he wore a gold wedding band on his left hand. His freckled face had a friendly look. The deciding factor was the mop of red hair, brushed sideways in a halfhearted attempt to cover a bald patch. *If you're betwixt and between, trust the one with red hair.*

He leaned over to open the passenger door.

"You can bung your haversack in the back. There's plenty of room," he said, misinterpreting her slowness.

"Oh. Yeah. Thanks."

Biting her lip, she got into the car.

"How far are you going?" he asked, as he eased back into traffic.

"The Burren. A place called Carron. It must be very small, it's not on my map."

"I know the spot. Near the University of Galway Field Station. Are you a student? Is that where you're staying?"

"No. Yes. Maybe. I don't know."

He gave her a curious glance but continued in his friendly manner.

"I can put you on the right road. My office is near Kilcolgan. You go west from there, through Kinvara on the way to Ballyvaughan, then south to Carron. Anyone will point out the way once you're in the Burren, though I wouldn't say your chance of a lift would be great. It's fairly barren country."

"I'll walk if I have to," she sighed.

He gave her another look, then frowned as if debating whether to speak or not.

"Is everything all right, pet?" he asked at last.

The kindness in his voice broke down her defenses. After all, he had the red hair that had been recommended to her, and she so wanted, needed, to confide in someone. In a rush of words, she told him about the night in Tara and how she had awakened to find her cousin gone. Then she explained that she was following the instructions of an odd little man. Though she avoided mentioning the words "fairy" or "leprechaun," she could still hear how crazy it sounded. When she was finished, she wondered what she would do if he insisted on taking her to a hospital or police station.

After a long pause, the businessman spoke quietly.

"Brave girls to sleep in a mound, but foolhardy too. There's no doubt about it, the fairies have taken her."

Despite all that had happened, Gwen was shocked.

"You believe in fairies?!"

He laughed, a rich warm sound that was pleasant to hear.

"Are they any less likely than angels or saints or Himself for that matter? I thought you looked a bit touched, but when I heard the accent I was sure I was mistaken."

"You mean this kind of thing happens all the time?!"

"Oh God no. But there was an old man in the village I was reared in who was taken by the fairies when he was young. To play a hurling match for them. He was the best hurler in the parish. He was never quite the same afterwards. Had that look about him—not quite here, not quite there. I remember it, still, after all these years. When I saw you, it put me in mind of him."

Gwen shuddered. She was not at all happy with the idea of looking "touched."

He was aware that she was upset. "Have you eaten?"

he asked. "We have a company cafeteria. Hot and cold buffet."

"That would be great," she said, cheered by the mention of food. "I'm Gwen Woods, by the way."

"Pleased to meet you, Gwen. Mattie O'Shea at your service."

They drove up the avenue of a company head office. Glass doors and wide windows gleamed in a façade of new brick. A rainbow of cars filled the parking lot.

"Not again!"

Mattie swore as he spied the sheep grazing on the front lawn. A few had already made their way to the flower beds and were nosing among the roses. He parked the car hurriedly and jumped out to chase the culprits. After shooing them back into a nearby field, he used branches to block the gap in the hedge where they had come in.

By the time he returned to Gwen, he was puffing from his exertions and mopping his face with a handkerchief. His red hair sprouted in all directions though he did his best to tamp it down.

She didn't know whether to laugh or sympathize.

"*Is glas iad na cnoic i bhfad uainn,*" he said with a grin. "The grass is always greener on the other side of the hill."

At the main entrance to the building, he held the door open for her in gentlemanly fashion. Waving to the receptionist, he ushered Gwen down the corridor. In the cafeteria, he nodded to various employees having their lunch.

"What a lucky coincidence you picked me up," Gwen said, as he handed her a meal ticket.

"There's no such thing as coincidence, pet. It was a complicated set of events that made me late for work today, including a mislaid report and a slow puncture, but I wouldn't hesitate to say that I was put in the right place at the right time to give you a hand. There are rules and traditions that govern the mingling of the fairy folk with our kind. They'll help you as much as hinder you. But it's a shame, now, that we aren't near my home in Kerry. I could find you a fairy doctor. That's what they call the local wise man or wise woman who has 'the cure' for various ailments and who knows the ways of the Good People. Not too many of them left nowadays, but they still exist. Like the fairies themselves."

He let out one of his deep laughs.

"I can tell you this, Gwen. Pay attention to any voices you might hear out of the blue. Don't think yourself mad. If you do cross over into Faerie, take no food or drink or you'll come under their sway. Most of all, keep your wits about you. With the fey folk, you'll always get more than you bargained for."

He glanced at his watch.

"Good Lord, I've a sales meeting in three minutes. Eat all around you. The food's on the house. I'll ask my secretary to drop you off on the road to Kinvara. I'm sorry I can't be of more help, but here's my card. Don't be afraid to ring me if you're in trouble."

"Thanks so much. You've been really great."

Overwhelmed by his kindness, Gwen gave him a hug.

Mattie blushed furiously.

He laughed. "You'll have the whole place talking about me. Good luck to you now."

He was halfway out the door when he hurried back to her.

"I was just thinking. The fairy folk don't have as much power as they used to. There's not much scope for them in a modern country. I'm wondering how they could have taken your cousin. Is she Irish?"

"Yes. Both parents. My mom is Irish too, but not my dad."

"That explains one thing," he said pensively, "but not the other."

"What?" she asked, catching his concern.

"I doubt they could have taken her if she didn't want to go."

Gwen caught her breath. Here was a complication she hadn't considered, perhaps because she didn't want to. Findabhair may not have been "stolen" in the true sense of the word. And now Gwen realized something else she had kept from herself. Finding Findabhair was not the sole reason for her search. Deep inside was the secret hurt that she, too, had not been spirited away.

Mattie was watching her closely. There was understanding in his voice as he warned her.

"You must take care, my dear. Even as you try to save your cousin, be certain of your motives. Otherwise both of you could be lost forever."

Gwen mulled over his words as she tucked into a generous portion of shepherd's pie with mushy marrowfat peas. She was just finishing her dessert of blackcurrant tart and fresh cream when Mattie's secretary arrived. An older woman with permed hair and glasses, she was casually dressed in slacks and blouse.

"Don't rush yourself," she said.

"I'm ready, thanks. I hope this isn't an inconvenience."

"Not at'all. I like to get away from my desk."

In the car, Gwen asked about Mattie's position in the company.

"He's the boss. The managing director. Didn't you know?"

Gwen was surprised.

"He must be very nice to work for."

"The best there is. Not like the crowd who ran the place before him. We were closing down with all jobs lost, when Mattie got the workers together to buy shares and keep the place going. He was the sales rep before, now he's the top man. More power to him."

Gwen was let off at a junction and shown the road to go. As the car drove away, the loneliness settled upon her once more. She had enjoyed having company. Still, a bubble of optimism welled up inside her. All by herself she had traveled west, made a new friend, and scrounged a good meal. Now she was well on her way to catch up with Findabhair. Everything was going to work out fine. In a country where bosses chased sheep off their lawns and talked about fairies as if they lived next door, what could go wrong?

SEVEN

The Burren was a craggy tableland embedded in the green countryside like a stone. Formed by glaciers aeons ago, the great terraces of limestone lay open for miles. Over time they had been scored and rilled by rain, till the fluted patterns of karren rippled like a sea of gray-blue stone. Rising above the lunar landscape were stepped hills, slippery steeps, the rugged defile of Glencolumkille, and the cliffs of Slievecarron. With the coming of spring, the rock garden bloomed. From every crack and crevice they peeped; blue gentian, mountain aven, the red bloody cranesbill, hart's-tongue, madder, purple helleborine, and a dazzling array of miniature orchids. By summer, the air was bright with butterflies.

Into this bubble of speckled stone, Gwen arrived on foot. As Mattie had predicted, she had no trouble traveling through County Clare, but once inside the Burren she was on her own. The solitude was unnerving. After an hour's hike, she had yet to meet another soul. On every side were barren fields with nothing but hazel scrub.

Some had barbed wire fencing, but most were bound by stone walls interwoven like lace. She knew she was on the right track. Occasional signposts pointed to Carron, but even without them she would have been confident. If ever a place was ideal for fairies, this terrain was it. So wild and forsaken, so strange and beautiful.

Reaching a crossroads, she came to a public house called *Croíde na Boirne*, "the heart of the Burren." Cool and dim inside, it was plainly furnished with wooden tables and benches. The smell of stale smoke hung in the air. Only two people were there, an old man at the counter sipping black stout and the young boy who served behind the bar.

Gwen bought a cola and a packet of peanuts.

"Is this Carron?" she asked the boy.

"It is. Are you looking for the Quirkes' house?"

"Who? No," she said uncertainly. "Is there a place around here where someone would hold a banquet?"

The old man coughed into his pint, while the boy fought to keep a straight face.

"You're some ways from a fancy hotel," he said. "There's one in Kinvara. But if you need a place to stop, you could try the Field Station. Through the village and first turn on your right. Students do stay there."

She heard them snickering as she left.

"A banquet hall no less," the old man said. "They're not the full shilling, them Yanks."

Despite their derision, Gwen felt hopeful. She was

near enough to what she sought, with a few hours yet to find it. Twilight was the appointed time and the sky was still bright. With renewed resolve, she set off once again down the road. Perhaps someone at the Field Station would be able to help.

But when she found the building standing alone outside Carron, it was closed and empty. She stared around in dismay. As far as the eye could see, stone walls and stony fields and low stony mountains stretched out on all sides. A strong wind blew over the landscape with a soft hollow roar, as if the rocks were hawing. Exhausted, downhearted, she almost roared back.

And, if the situation weren't bad enough, she was starving.

She was about to turn back for the village, when she heard a sound overhead. Her name echoed on the air.

"What?"

She shielded her eyes to look up.

Wings beat the wind as a sparrow hawk dove.

"Hey, watch it!" she yelled, ducking down.

She was glad no one was around. Talking to birds! Then she remembered Mattie's advice. *Pay attention to any voices you might hear out of the blue.* She searched the sky for the hawk.

It hovered over a field nearby. Then with a raucous screech it swooped. Something caught? No, something called. A fox streaked out from the underbrush. Jumping over a stone wall, it landed daintily on the road in front of

Gwen. The fiery tail flicked back and forth as the eyes stared at her brazenly. Were those tiny silver rings in his elegant ears? She didn't get the chance to look closer. With a final swish of his tail, the fox raced away.

Gwen didn't stop to think. She immediately ran after.

Before long she was scrambling over walls and through stony fields. The ground was treacherous. Where the gullies deepened to grykes, she had to jump across openings big enough to swallow her. The weight of her knapsack didn't help. It felt as if it were packed with rocks. At times she was caught in briary patches that scraped and scratched her. Though she tried to watch where she was going, the inevitable occurred. Her foot caught in a crack and she tripped. In a spectacular fall, she landed on her hands and knees with a smack. The pain was like a burn. The wind was knocked out of her. Dazed, she lay at the edge of a crevice and peered into the dimness. She could see a profusion of ferns and flowers below, like a tiny forest. Could these fissures be entrances to an underworld? There was no time to investigate. Ahead, the fox barked. *Hurry up*, it seemed to say.

Gwen hauled herself to her feet. Rubbing her palms to soothe the sting, she spotted her quarry. On she ran.

At first she tried to keep track of the way, noting landmarks and any distinctive features, but in the end she hiked blindly just to keep up. Sometimes the fox disappeared, leaving her lost and alone. A gloom would fall over her. What on earth was she doing? Why was she chasing a wild animal? Then his head would pop up, a splash of red against the gray of rock, and she was off again. Her throat grew parched. She felt light-headed. The constant glare of sun on stone hurt her eyes. But she had long passed any notion of giving up. It was as if she were driven in her pursuit of him.

The chase ended as abruptly as it had begun. The fox came to the jagged face of a cliff. The incline appeared unscalable, a sheer rise overlaid with scree. Nevertheless, the fox scurried upward.

Gwen's heart sank. She knew she couldn't do it. Weak with hunger and fatigue, she felt the ground sway beneath her feet. The landscape was askew.

The fox stopped only once to look back at her. The silver rings in his ears glinted in the sunlight. His gaze seemed to show disappointment. Was she hallucinating? There was a buzzing sound in her head. Then, with a hail of loose stones in his wake, he disappeared over the top of the ridge.

Gwen was too sick and dizzy to care. Staggering along a stone wall that eventually led to the road, she came upon an open gate. Exhausted, she leaned against it for support. The iron railings felt cool. She closed her eyes.

When the shouts rang out, she didn't react right away.

The cries came from the next field up. A farmer was waving to her from a stone enclosure. Cows were ambling out of the pen and making their way toward her.

"Stand fast to herd them!" the farmer called again.

With horror, Gwen realized that the cattle were head-ing for the gate. A true city girl, she had no experience with farm animals and found the size of cows terrifying. Frozen to the spot, not knowing what to do, she was cer-tain they were going to stampede and kill her.

The first to arrive was a black-and-white bullock. It barely acknowledged Gwen as it loped out the gate and down the road. The next did the same, and on followed the rest, till Gwen saw that she was sending them in the right direction simply by standing there.

Accompanied by a sheepdog, the farmer came last. She was a young woman in her early twenties, dressed in a faded shirt and muddied denims with wellington boots. An old cap rested on her mass of red hair. In her hand she carried a hazel switch, occasionally thwacking the rear ends of any cattle that strayed.

"Thanks for the hand," she said brightly to Gwen. "This lazy thing should have been doing the job, but he's too tired to run ahead sometimes. Ready for your pen-sion, aren't you, Bran?"

She scratched the ears of the dog, who whined apolo-getically. Then she put out her hand to shake Gwen's.

"Kathleen Quirke. Call me Katie or call me quirky. Are you on your way to my house?"

Gwen introduced herself. "I don't know. They asked me that in the pub too. Do you run a hostel?"

Katie laughed. She was a handsome strong-featured girl with hazel eyes full of humor and intelligence. Taller than Gwen, lean and tanned from outdoor work, she exuded health and high spirits.

"You could call it that. We take in 'woofers'—Willing Workers on Organic Farms. They're always arriving on the doorstep, Americans, Germans, Italians, English. They work on the farm and we feed and house them."

"Only foreigners? No Irish?"

Katie snorted. "You wouldn't catch the Irish working for nothing. They've more sense. Have you got a light? I'm down to my last match and saving it."

"Sorry, I don't smoke."

"Neither do I. Much."

Katie took a half-used butt from her shirt pocket and cupped her hands to protect the flame of her match. Some of the cows had wandered up the road, but most stood nibbling the grass on the verge, waiting patiently for their mistress. She looked set for a long and leisurely conversation, but Gwen put an end to that by tilting forward in a near faint.

Katie caught her.

"What's the matter?" she demanded, all concern.

"I . . . I'm okay," Gwen said, steadying herself. But her face was pale. "It's just that I haven't eaten for a while and I've been walking for miles."

"You poor thing!"

Ignoring Gwen's protests, Katie slung the girl's knapsack over her own shoulders as easily as if it weighed nothing at all.

"The house isn't far. We'll soon fix you up. Lean on me and we'll go all the faster."

"Sorry to be such a nuisance," Gwen said miserably.

"Don't be silly. I'd be a poor Christian if it were a bother to help someone."

Together they made their way up the road, Katie herding the cattle ahead as they went.

"We're nearly there now. I'll just hunt these lads into the *Maher Buídhe* and we'll be home in a tick."

The Quirke homestead was a big thatched farmhouse on the side of a mountain. A straggle of white goats wandered in the front yard where a rusty tractor stood idle. A walled garden at the side sheltered apple trees and rows of vegetables. Behind the house were a cattle yard, sheds, and an open hay barn.

"The car's gone," Katie commented, looking around. "Mam and the girls must be counting sheep."

The front door opened into a broad shady living room dominated by a fireplace with dark-red flagstones. Woven panniers stood on each side of the hearth, filled with sods of peat. In the center of the room was a great round table with a crocheted lace cloth and a vase of sunflowers. The television was perched on top of an old piano. Rugs were scattered over the floor, in front of the stuffed sofa and armchairs. On the walls were photographs of the family, going back generations.

Gwen felt embraced by a sense of "home."

"Sit you down while I get us a bite," Katie ordered, heading for the kitchen.

She returned with a feast of cold ham and beef, home-made goat's cheese, creamed potato salad, and a plate of brown bread. The two ate hungrily without a word, washing down the meal with mugs of tea.

Gwen sat back with a sigh, completely revived.

"That's better." Katie grinned with satisfaction. "You were white as a ghost. I thought you were going to faint on me. I'd've had to put you up on the black Limousin. He's pure wild. Might have run off with you into the mountains."

She let out a laugh, but Gwen looked puzzled.

"Limousine? I didn't see a car."

Katie spluttered, laughing louder.

"A Limousin is a breed of cattle. You're a right eejit."

Gwen laughed too. She didn't mind Katie making fun of her. The older girl was already something of a heroine to her.

"I don't know how to thank you," she began.

Katie waved away her words.

"Listen, you're to stop here tonight and get a good rest. You can help me with a few things tomorrow before going on your way, or you can stay as long as you like. We'll make a woofer out of you. What do you say to that?"

Gwen thought it sounded wonderful—to become friends with Katie and meet her family, to work outdoors on the farm, maybe in the garden, or even with the animals. Just to stay in one place for a while, instead of roaming around the country all by herself!

"I'd love to, believe me," she said ruefully, "but I can't. It's hard to explain. I was traveling with my cousin and she . . . we . . . got split up. I'm supposed to meet her somewhere around here, but the . . . um . . . arrangements are sort of vague . . ."

Katie listened sympathetically.

"You had a row? That's bound to happen when two people travel together. Don't worry, you'll be friends when you meet up again. A little time away makes all the difference."

Gwen nodded guiltily, without explaining further. She wasn't about to mention fairies to someone near her own age. Mattie was different, being much older. At the same time, she didn't like deceiving her new friend and she did her best not to lie.

"Here's the problem. How will I find my cousin? There's supposed to be some kind of banquet tonight, near Carron. Not a modern place, I think. Something old or ancient? That's what we've been touring around to see."

"There's Leamanagh," Katie suggested. "Máire Ruadh's great house. She was the wife of an O'Brien chieftain who was killed in the Cromwellian wars. She married an English officer so her sons could keep their land. The castle isn't far from here, but it's a ruin. It couldn't host a feast like the sort they have at Bunratty.

Something ancient," she muttered to herself. Then her face lit up. "What about the *Fulacht Fia*! Could that be it? The Ancient Eating Place on the Boston Road. It's just outside the village. You must have passed it."

"Ancient Eating Place?" Gwen thought a moment. "That could be it. It's certainly worth checking. I'm sorry to be rude, but I'll clean up and then go. I'm supposed to be there by twilight!"

Katie caught her urgency and glanced out the window. The sun was setting over the Burren, inflaming the stone mountains.

"Never mind the dishes, we'll wash up later. We can go on my motorbike. Come on!"

Eight

The motorbike bucked and leaped like a colt as Katie sped down the road heedless of the potholes. Behind her, Gwen clung on for dear life as they dipped into curves and skimmed past walls. The sun was low in the sky. Was she too late? When exactly was twilight? As they turned into a narrow lane not far from Carron, Gwen recognized the spot where the sparrow hawk had called her. Did the bird and the fox lead her astray? She made a mental note not to be so trusting. She would have to stop being an "eejit" as Katie would say.

They drew up at a lonely signpost pointing into an empty field.

FULACHT FIA. ANCIENT EATING PLACE.

"There isn't much to see," Katie said, removing her helmet. "Just a grassy circle and a few stones. It would have been where a Celtic tribe feasted together."

"Or some other 'tribe,'" Gwen murmured.

"Are you sure your cousin will come? What if this isn't the right place? I'll wait with you."

"*No!*" said Gwen, with more force than she intended. She rushed out her words to fend off Katie's dismay. "It's not that I don't appreciate your offer, but this is something I have to do alone."

The older girl was not convinced. She pointed to the dark clouds that were gathering over the mountains.

"There'll be a storm tonight. They're pure wild in the summertime. I'm not going to leave you here —"

"You don't know what's going on!" Gwen said in a panic, sensing that Katie might dig in her heels. "I hardly know myself. It could be dangerous. I can't drag you into it."

Gwen saw immediately that she had taken the wrong tack. Katie's eyes flashed. She was the impulsive kind, ready for action. Very like Findabhair in fact. That made up Gwen's mind. She didn't need another one lost in Faerie.

"No," said Gwen again, in a quiet and final tone. "The farm needs you. Your family needs you. I won't argue any more, but you've got to understand. This is my battle. Please let me handle it myself."

She had gotten it right this time. Katie gave in, albeit reluctantly.

"Fair enough. We all have our patch to plow. I won't interfere with yours. Good luck to you, then, with whatever it is you're facing. I gather you haven't told me everything, but that's your business. Remember now, if you need me, you know where I am."

As the motorbike disappeared down the road, Gwen

felt a pang of regret. She would have liked to have had Katie with her. Still, she felt it was the right decision.

A wooden stile brought her into the field. She followed a trail through the damp grass. It led her to a green hollow circled by white stones half-buried in the earth. Removing her knapsack, she sat down to wait.

Darkness settled over the Burren. Above was scattered a handful of stars. A cool wind blew from the shadow of the mountains. In the deep quiet and stillness, Gwen acknowledged the truth. She had strayed far from the path. She was out beyond the walls in the uncharted night. Could she brave it? Despite her fear, she didn't move. She was determined to face whatever might come.

When it happened, it happened immediately, as if the other world had shaken itself awake with a roar.

Their arrival was like a blast of wind, a great soft blow. They poured into the hollow like molten silver. Almost indescribable in human terms. Almost invisible to mortal eyes. Their silhouettes hinted of slender graceful shapes, but they were so amorphous as to appear also like streams or columns of falling light. They were translucent, and transparent too, for Gwen could see through them to the contours of the landscape. Did they have wings? Or was that moonlight trailing behind them? They moved with such breathtaking swiftness that wings, pale limbs, and tresses all blended together.

Paralyzed, Gwen sat wide-eyed and watching. She was seized by a wonder that was also terror. These were not human, not of the world she knew. Their very existence was shattering. Unable to stop herself, she uttered a cry.

Their madcap movements ceased abruptly. Trembling like moonbeams, the glorious creatures stood still.

"There is a mortal amongst us!"

The cry wailed on the wind.

"What brought this human here?"

The hiss was like water dousing flame.

Gwen wanted to answer, to explain and apologize, but she felt so heavy beside their lightness, like a dull lump of stone or a sod of earth. Sphinxlike she sat, solemn and dumbstruck, staring into eyes that stared back like stars.

They gathered around her, peering into her face. She felt crowded by moonlight and will-o'-the-wisps. Some patted her curiously with gentle strokes. One blew into her mouth and ears. She quivered at their touch, but couldn't move or speak.

"She has not seen us before. She is *fairy-struck*."

Their whisperings rustled like leaves in a tree. They were calmer now as they saw she was helpless.

"A golden-haired girl," someone said softly, "with a face as pale as the moon."

"She is a pretty mortal."

"Shall we take her with us?"

"Here is our captain!"

"He will know."

Though Gwen could barely discern one shape from another—they all flashed and flickered like fireworks—she was able to see the tall youth who approached her. His red-gold hair fell to his shoulders. His eyes were as blue as a summery sea. His ears were pierced with silver rings. As if in a dream, she wondered why he seemed familiar and she was all the more confused when he spoke her name.

"Fair Gwenhyvar, wilst thou come to our banquet?"

The word "banquet" was like a charm that set her free. With a gasp, she surfaced from her stupor and jumped to her feet.

"Where is my cousin?" she demanded.

The shining youth shook his head.

"She is not here, fair one. My name is Midir. I tried to guide you to our palace, but you did not follow me to the door in the mountain. Thus have I come with my troop to aid you."

Gwen was about to thank him, when she changed her mind. Hadn't she promised herself to stop being naïve?

"Why are you helping me?" she asked instead.

He seemed bemused by her question.

"You denied the King when he came for you." Wonder echoed through his words. "No mortal woman has ever resisted him."

Gwen shuffled uneasily. His gaze was so intense she could feel herself blushing.

"Well," she said, "there's a first time for everything."

His laughter was a spell in itself. Charmed, she had to laugh too.

"There is nothing more exciting than a challenge," he said. "Don't you agree?"

Without waiting for her answer, the fairy captain shot into the sky. His voice rang out to command the night.

"Get me a horse!"

Now the rest of his troop took up the cry.

"Come fairy steeds from the Cave of the Wild Horses!"

Their shouts resounded over the Burren to the cave in which the fairy steeds dwelt. Out came the wild horses from their craggy stable, like a rush of wind rolling down the mountains.

Gwen saw them in the clouds, racing past the moon. Arched necks and broad chests and huge eyes like opals. Some were black as the night, others white as the moonlight. One had golden-brown hair, the same color as her own. Stars glittered in their manes, which swept behind them like wings. Hooves thundered across the sky. They galloped towards the fairy folk, tossing their heads and snorting defiantly. Did anyone dare ride them?

The fairies were quick to respond. They raced to the horses. Some succeeded in mounting with one fleet jump. Others were flung away to somersault in the air like fiery pinwheels. Still others, unable to take their seats, ran alongside, arms entangled in horse hair, screeching with laughter and mock pleas for mercy.

Gwen quaked inside. This wild abandon, this utter madness, was beyond anything she could imagine. It was a nightmare she had no hope of handling. Exquisite chaos. Again she was overwhelmed by the terrifying truth. All these beings, both riders and steeds, were supernatural. They shouldn't exist.

And yet, something inside her, some vague, restless, and exiled part of her, recognized them. Remembered them. In the deep ocean of her unconscious, the dreamer stirred. She wavered between the fear of what might happen if she joined them, and the equal fear of being left behind.

No kind hand was proffered to help her mount. She knew in her heart she had to do this alone.

Courage is not a lack of fear. It is acting despite the fear.

The words whispered inside her. Her soul fluttered like a bird in its cage, yearning to be free.

Now she made a dash for the high-stepping mare with the golden-brown mane.

"You are for me!" she cried.

The horse reared up, but as soon as the hooves touched the earth again Gwen saw her chance. Leaping forward to grasp the mane, she flung a leg over the shining bare back. The mare bucked ferociously to toss her away. Half-up, half-down, Gwen flapped in midair like a paper bag in the wind. She gripped so tightly her knuckles went white. But she couldn't keep her hold. The horse's hair began to slip through her fingers. Straining, clutching, she strove to hang on.

To no avail. With a cry of anguish, she lost her grip and fell to the ground. She rolled out of control. By the time she came to a stop, flat on her back, she was bruised and battered.

Gwen choked back her tears as she stared up at the sky. She was utterly humiliated. There they were, far above her, the fairy troop on horseback, glittering in the night like a spray of stars. She would never forget the look in their eyes as they gazed down on her. So cool and distant. Such breathtaking indifference!

At the head of the troop rode Midir on a red-gold steed. His own fiery mane was a comet's tail behind him. Did she imagine the regret she saw in his glance? But he didn't look back when he sped away, any more than the rest of them. All simply abandoned her there in the dark.

That's when something snapped in Gwen.

"No!" she cried after them. "Don't go without me! *Not again!*"

She scrambled to her feet, looking around wildly. The golden-brown mare had not gone far and appeared to be grazing innocently. But Gwen could see the tension in her limbs.

"You are for me!" Gwen called again, gritting her teeth. "If it takes all night!"

Now she ran for the horse even as the mare prepared to bolt. Gwen was quicker, spurred by a furious need to rejoin the troop. Once more she leaped at the horse's back to grasp the long mane. Once more she dangled helplessly in midair. Once more she clung on with all her might. The moment seemed to stretch into forever, an unrelenting eternity of cold wind, torn fingers, and battered body. But this time she refused to let go. This time she drew on the last ounce of her strength, the last breath in her lungs. She would not let go, even if it meant being trampled to death.

Sensing the iron will of her hapless rider, the fairy steed grew calm.

In that moment of sweet stillness Gwen righted herself. She patted the mare's neck with relief and respect.

"Thank you, lady," she whispered into an elegant ear.

The mare whinnied in response and flew into the sky.

It wasn't long before Gwen caught up with the fairy troop as they raced across the heavens. Her heart skipped a beat at Midir's smile of approval. Then the others let out a jubilant shout.

"Ride fast! Ride fast! The spell is cast!"

Πίπε

Oh, the exhilaration of that night ride over the Burren! Silver-shod hooves rode the currents of air like the smooth sward of a plain. *Wild and bitter is the wind tonight.* Triumphantly one of the glorious host, Gwen felt like a goddess. *We come from the Land of the Ever-Living where there is neither pain nor sorrow.* Her eyes shone with fairy sight as she gazed on the landscape below. *Transient is the splendor of your world, eternal is ours.*

Over Cahercommaun they flew. An ancient stone fort on the edge of a cliff, it no longer stood as a ruin in modern time. Smoke curled from within the high ramparts. A proud people dwelled in the great hall of stone. Cloaks of bright linen fell from their shoulders, clasped with gold brooches. Torcs brighter than the sun glimmered at their throats. Both men and women were of a noble bearing, fierce and unbowed.

"All hail!" cried the fairies as they passed by. "All hail to the Celtic tribes of Erin!"

Perishable are the hosts of short-lived mortals. Your life is as brief and swift as a whisper.

On they sped to Leamanagh Castle where lights sparkled in the mullioned windows. At a banquet table laden with meats and wine, Máire Ruadh dined her Saxon guest. Unbowed by defeat, she wooed the conqueror with a toss of her long red hair. In the passage of time her plans would succeed. Her sons would be chieftains like their murdered father.

"Our blessings upon you, lionhearted Mary!"

Onward again dashed the cavalcade, beneath the sky of stars. Over cairn and cashel, over bog and rushy pasture, over runneled rock meadow and holy well. *We do not wish to settle, we do not care to sleep.* From their marvelous height they could see everything, even the secrets that lay under the earth. Subterranean rivers streamed through labyrinthine caves. Stalactites pierced the dark underworld air. The black waters of turloughs seeped up through the limestone to glimmer in the moonlight.

When they reached the majestic Poulnabrone Dolmen, standing alone in a stony field, the fairies swooped down. Inside the sheltering walls of the cromlech, two young lovers lay asleep. Their beauty was marred by hunger and hardship, but they dreamed of a lasting future together. Neither regretted the love that had made them fugitives from the warriors of the Fianna and Finn MacCumhail.

A hush fell over the fairy folk as they approached the

dolmen. All were solemn-eyed like worshippers at a way-side shrine. They laid gifts of food at the lovers' feet and covered their cold limbs with sheepskin rugs.

Sweet Diarmuid and Gráinne. We who were ancient in ancient days grant thee a night's peace from the din of men and the hunters' hounds.

The young couple stirred in each other's arms and smiled in their sleep.

Airborne once more, Gwen was ready to ride forever. *Come away, O human child!* She had discarded all memory of her former life. She had forgotten her own name. There was only the night wind and the flight of the wild horses and the company of a shining angelic folk. *Come away to the bright-edged strand of the world.*

They soared over a farmhouse on the side of a mountain. With a start, Gwen recognized the thatched roof of the Quirke homestead. Bran was asleep on the doorstep, but he suddenly lifted his head to bay. Inside, the family turned in their beds as they, too, sensed the Hosting of the *Sídhe* pass by.

For Gwen, it was a nudge from her past. A discomfiting reminder.

"I'm human," she whispered, both sad and surprised.

A warning sounded faintly in the back of her mind. A man's voice echoing from far away.

You must take care, my dear. Otherwise both of you could be lost forever.

Now the fairy troop began to descend toward a steep

cliffside. As they plummeted downward, Gwen recognized the ridge to which the fox had led her. They were dropping so fast she was certain they would crash. Then she saw the crack in the side of the mountain.

With a rush of wings and wind, they sailed inside.

There was a moment, before the troop dismounted, when Gwen suffered the sensation that all was not as it seemed. The crevice they had entered appeared suddenly minute, an opening for creatures as small as insects. Her sight wavered. The fairy steeds looked like dragonflies!

"Is this a dream?" she wondered.

Midir came to lift her down from her horse. The firm grip of his hands around her waist steadied her.

"What's real and what isn't?" she asked him.

The summer-blue eyes were bright with laughter.

"The order of things is ours to play with. We can create a sun and a moon. The heavens we can sprinkle with radiant stars of the night. Wine we can make from the cold waters of the Boyne, sheep from stones, and swine from fern. On the mortal plane, life is a web of illusion. We weave what we wish."

They were standing in a souterrain lit by torches. At the end of the long passageway was a flight of steps that led downward. The other fairies had run ahead, laughing and chattering among themselves. No longer shadowy beings of light, they appeared, like their captain, to be solid and human. Like him also, they were strikingly beautiful.

Midir offered Gwen his arm.

She hung back, uncertain. For all his charm, she didn't trust him. Was she a pawn in some fairy game? He might abduct her as the King had done her cousin.

But when he spoke, he sounded sincere.

"Do not fear and no harm will befall you. Only take no food or wine that may be offered to you, if you wish to return to your world again."

In the end, she went with him. What other choice did she have?

He led her down the steps, deep into the mountain. The rock walls were ribbed and muscled like a torso. The musky scent of clay caught at her throat. The tintinnabulation of trickling water chimed through the dimness. Deeper and deeper they went, till the lights disappeared and they were walking into darkness. *Over wave and over fountain. Under hill and under mountain.* Her grip on Midir's arm tightened. She was beginning to fear she would never see daylight again.

Then they came to an archway with a great bronze door that opened into the hollow heart of the mountain.

And the fairy tale began anew.

The cavern was of breathtaking grandeur and beauty. Its vast floors gleamed a royal purple, smooth porphyry inlaid with crystals of amethyst. Marble pillars rose to the high ceiling to be lost in the recesses. A thousand white candles illumined the gallery. Elaborate tapestries draped the walls, their needlework depicting a land of enchantment.

Fruitful is every fair field in blossom. The salmon leap in stony streams. Across the full waters glide winged swans. Ever green are the tangled groves of holly. Honey-gold are the woods. At eventide, the sun sends down its red shafts from out of the west. And strange birds nest in the apple trees.

Gwen found herself thinking of the Garden of Eden. Did the fairies still have what her own race had lost? But there was little time to muse. Her senses were being bombarded by every kind of marvel.

The bright assembly of the Court was as splendid as the hall. Of every exquisite shape, size, and color, the fairies were resplendent in lavish fashion. There were flounces of silk and the sheen of satin, brocaded cloths stitched with gold-wrapped thread, rich dark velvets trimmed with pearls, and tasseled trains of lustrous damask. Every throat, arm, and wrist was ablaze with rubies, sapphires, and emeralds. Every head was adorned with tiaras or jeweled caps and combs.

Gwen blinked with astonishment. Never had she seen such extravagance! She would have stood there gaping all night, if Findabhair hadn't come running.

"You got here! Well done, cuz! I thought that rascal might play tricks on you. The King, I mean. I had no way of reaching you. We've been on the move since Tara. God, it's been madness. Parties day and night. These people are daft. I feel like I've died and gone to heaven!"

"So, you're okay."

Ten

Gwen had only to look at her cousin to see that she was no suffering captive. In a gown of midnight-black filigreed with silver, Findabhair looked like a young queen. Her long hair, more golden now, was plaited in four locks with a diamond drop at each end. Eyes sparkling with laughter, cheeks flushed like two roses, she was obviously having the time of her life.

Her high spirits plunged at Gwen's cool reception, and she was immediately contrite.

"Has it been hard for you? Oh Gwen, I'm so sorry. I agreed to go without thinking. I had no idea you wouldn't come too!"

Gwen couldn't speak. Too many things crowded into her mind and onto her tongue at the same time. How could her cousin be so selfish and self-centered? Had she given no thought to Gwen at all? And what might be happening to her? All the hardship Gwen had faced, searching frantically for her, the loneliness of the long road, the fairy trickeries, not to mention the constant worry in the back of her mind.

Is Findabhair safe? Is Findabhair suffering? And here she was, all dressed up and having a ball!

At the same time—and in all fairness, Gwen admitted this—the adventure around Ireland had been truly exciting. She had surprised herself by doing so well on her own. And the friends she had made were well worth the trouble.

So why was she upset? Why this simmer of anger?

"What do you mean I wouldn't come too?" she demanded.

Aware that something was wrong between them, Findabhair spoke frankly.

"Finvarra said so. The King of the Fairies. His name is like mine, isn't that brilliant? Apparently my spirit agreed to go wholeheartedly—what can I say, that's me—but you resisted. By fairy law, he couldn't take you. He was very annoyed, let me tell you, as he wanted the two of us, the cheeky thing. Fairies are not monogamous by any stretch of the imagination."

Findabhair burst out laughing. Gwen had to grin. Her cousin was "pure wild," as Katie would say. But it was what she had said that assuaged Gwen's feelings, for it removed the hurt she had secretly nursed inside. So, she hadn't been left behind! The fairy folk didn't reject her! It was her own nature that kept her back. Gwen's grin widened as she understood.

"I'm just too practical to jump 'wholeheartedly' into Gagaland."

As they laughed together, the tension between them eased.

"You're still in black. You look terrific." Gwen frowned at her own muddied clothes, so out of place in the gorgeous surroundings.

"Finvarra loves black too," said Findabhair, "being Lord of the Night and all. Say a color—not pink or I'll gag—and I'll work a bit of magic on you."

"Can you really?" Gwen was skeptical, but it was worth a try. "Well, if I can't have pink, how about a passionate red and some of that silver stuff you've got?"

"Excellent! You're getting more daring, old girl."

With a mischievous grin, Findabhair waved her hand.

Gwen gasped at the transformation. Clouds of fiery satin floated around her. The bodice and sleeves were stippled with pearls. More pearls dripped from her ears and throat. Her feet were shod with ruby slippers.

"Wow! How did you do that?"

"Fairy glamour," said her cousin, with a nonchalant shrug. "None of this is real, you know. We could be standing here starkers."

"Thanks. I needed that thought like a hole in the head."

But Gwen wasn't going to worry about the finer details. She felt like Cinderella who had finally gotten to the ball, and she was going to make the most of it before her time ran out!

Now it was Findabhair's turn to be serious. Catching Gwen's arm, she drew her away to a secluded corner of the hall.

"Listen, we need to talk before Finvarra makes his grand entrance. I don't want him to overhear."

"'Disenchanted' already, are we?"

"Ha ha. But this is no joke, Gwen. He's a tricky divil. Don't underestimate him. He thinks he's God's gift to women, so I'm cooling his heels. It's not easy, I really fancy him, and I'm beginning to think the feeling's mutual. But I can tell he's not happy that you escaped him. He's plotting against you. I don't know what or how, but you've got to be careful."

"Is this a big game or what?"

"*Life* is a game for the fairies, Gwen. Feasting and frolic, music and dancing. They've been here since the world began, but they never grow old and I'd say they never grow up."

"Permanent teenagers," Gwen said, in awe.

"That's it in a nutshell," Findabhair agreed. "And that's why I love them. But you have to keep in mind, they are not like us. They don't have the same kind of feelings. Guilt is something they know nothing about. That might be fine for some, but it means they can get away with murder without batting an eyelid."

"You seem to know them pretty well."

"To live with them is to know them," Findabhair

declared airily. Then she added, with a rueful grimace, "And I am their Queen, for what it's worth."

Gwen had to smile. "You might think I've changed, but you have too. You sound a lot more sensible."

"Hey, when everyone around you is cracked, you've got to keep a head on your shoulders." Now she lowered her voice, worried. "I'm serious about the warning, cuz. I can't put my finger on it, but there's something wrong. Under all this sweetness and light, I smell a rat. Something dark."

"*I, too, was the hostage,*" Gwen murmured, "*I, too, was the Hunted and the Sacrificed.*"

Findabhair's features froze.

"What did you say?"

Gwen shook her head, confused.

A strange gloom fell over the girls, and they both looked lost. Before either could say anything more, a fanfare of trumpets blared through the hall. The music and dancing ceased abruptly as the lords and ladies of the Court bowed low.

The King had arrived.

Dressed purely in black, a silken mantle tossed over his shoulders, he was a startling figure. His jet-black hair fell in a blunt cut to his shoulders, reminiscent of ancient Egypt. And like a pharaoh carved in stone, he had finely chiseled features, proud and exquisite. Though his garments glimmered darkly like the night, he wore no adornment save the sign of his sovereignty: the silver star that glittered upon his brow.

"My lord and master," Findabhair said wryly.

Despite the dry tone, Gwen could see that her cousin was barely keeping rein on a breathless excitement.

"Be careful yourself," she warned.

"Isn't he gorgeous but?"

"Not my type."

Gwen's attempt at indifference rang hollow, even to herself.

Dark and intense, the King's glance swept the hall. He spied them huddled in the corner like conspirators. For a split second, his gaze rested on Gwen. She felt seared by its force. When his attention moved on, she suffered the loss as a pang.

With an elegant gesture, the King extended his hand to Findabhair as melodious music rang out once more.

"Duty calls," said Findabhair. "I'm off!"

"Wait a minute! We've got to—"

But her cousin was already skipping away, catching up her skirts as she ran. Gwen watched, chagrined, as Findabhair melted into the King's embrace. The two twirled on the floor like figurines in a jewelry box.

Feeling awkward and abandoned, Gwen edged closer to a pillar to hide in its shadow. The misery of the wallflower. *Always the bridesmaid, never the bride.* She looked around for a buffet table, needing a place to stand where she might appear less alone.

"Lady, will you dance?"

Midir bowed before her. He wore a tunic of bronze-colored linen with a flowing green cloak. The earrings were gone, but golden brooches clasped his mantle. Gold, too, was the circlet that bound his fiery hair.

Gwen yearned to say yes, but she was overcome by shyness.

"I'm not very good. In fact, I'm hopeless. I never go dancing."

"It is not possible to stumble to fairy music," he assured her.

She consented at last, though with serious misgivings, certain that she was about to make a fool of herself. But Midir's words proved true. With his arm around her waist, guiding her effortlessly, she found herself gliding across the floor. With every step she took, her confidence grew. Now the music swept through her, a wild dash of a waltz. Soon she was whirling and twirling amid the bright throng. It was as if her feet had grown wings. She was dancing on air. She was flying!

"This is fabulous! I really feel like Cinderella."

"A charming girl. I remember her well."

"How could you? That's just a—"

"Fairy tale?"

They laughed together as they spun around the hall. It wasn't only the dancing that was new and exciting to Gwen, but talking freely with a handsome young man as well. Was everything easier in Faerie? If only she could be like this in her own world!

"Will this lady grant me a dance?" said a voice behind her.

Though she would have preferred to stay with Midir, Gwen didn't want to be rude.

"Okay," she said blithely, turning to face her next partner.

She nearly jumped with fright when she saw who it was. Ready or not, he caught hold of her.

Gwen was now dancing with the King of Faerie.

Eleven

Though she managed to keep her step, Gwen quaked inside. She wasn't sure what to do. He had caught her off guard. She could sense the immense power contained in his person, barely held in check. He was like a panther, sleek and dark. Ready to pounce.

Steady up, she ordered herself. She was annoyed that he could make her so nervous. A cool head was needed, or he would get the better of her.

"Fair Gwenhyvar, you have honored my court with your presence after all."

He spoke graciously.

Too graciously, she thought.

"No thanks to you or your tricksy leprechaun. If it wasn't for Midir, I could still be sitting in a dark field, like an ass."

A spark flared in the King's eyes. Gwen couldn't tell if it was anger or amusement.

"You are of the same mettle as Findabhair. I did not

think so when first I spied you at Tara. She was the bri-
ared rose and you, the buttercup."

"The story of my life."

That made him laugh, a rather delightful laugh, and
he touched her chin.

"I *love* butter," he said.

It was the last thing she expected, this irresistible
charm. Her defenses wobbled. She knew he was teasing
her and she couldn't help but laugh. Though she fought
hard against it, she was beginning to like him.

As if sensing the change in her, Finvarra smiled playfully.

"Perhaps you regret your refusal of me?"

"Maybe," she teased back, surprising herself.

This was flirting, wasn't it? Findabhair would kill
her. She scanned the hall quickly. Her cousin was dancing in the arms of a blond giant, laughing as if she hadn't
a care in the world. *Serves her right if the King likes me
too.* With horror she pushed the dark whisper away.

"I'm not into harems," she said, a little more loudly
than she intended. "It's not right."

The King's voice was smooth. "There is no such
thing as right or wrong in Faerie."

"Then it's not somewhere I want to be!"

She tried to sound adamant, to stand her ground, but
she was really in turmoil. She could feel herself slipping
under his sway, caught by his lure. To her great relief, the
dance came to an end.

He bowed farewell.

"I shall leave you to my *Tánaiste* who seems as intrigued by you as I. May I trust we are now on better terms?"

She stared into the catlike eyes that reflected the wisdom and wildness of millennia. It was impossible to deny him. When he kissed her on the cheek, she could only smile.

As soon as Finvarra left, Midir rejoined her. At his quizzical look, she shook her head.

"What can I say? I have met the enemy and he's Prince Charming."

"He is the King."

"And you're the *Tánaiste*? What does that mean?"

"I am his second-in-command. Though I am captain of my own troop and there are many like me, Finvarra is High King over all. If anything were to happen to him, I would rule in his place. But that is unlikely as we are, each of us, immortal."

Gwen caught her breath as his statement struck home. She was dancing with someone who would live forever! The concept was inconceivable, like grasping the size of the universe. She would have asked him more about fairy life, but a burst of fireworks exploded in the hall. Multicolored birds and sparkling butterflies lit up the air, along with blazing red dragons and Catherine wheels.

"It must be wonderful," she said, "to live with magic every day."

Midir's blue eyes lingered on her.

"I should like to have you always near me."

Something in his voice told her it was time to make her position clear, not only to him but to herself as well.

"I couldn't stay here. It's out of the question. Though the temptation is huge, believe me. This is all so weird. All I've ever dreamed of is escaping to other worlds and here I've found one, and it's incredibly beautiful . . . But now that it's offered to me, I know the truth. At the most, I only ever meant to visit. I mean, even though it's far from perfect, I never intended to reject my own life."

His look was wistful, but he nodded.

"I accept your decision, and I would not hold you against your will. But I cannot say the same of the King. More goes on here than meets the eye. You must take care."

That was the last straw for Gwen. She had had her fill of fairy games and intrigues.

"Look, what's the story here?" she demanded. "You've been very nice and I appreciate all your help, but instead of vague hints and warnings, why can't you just come out and tell me what's going on?"

She saw the veil fall over his features. His tone was guarded.

"I am of Faerie and the land of Faerie, and I am bound by its laws. It is easy enough for me to assist you, for I have the red hair that by our custom grants aid. Yet I cannot cross Finvarra directly. Though I am aware that he schemes against you, I am not privy to his designs.

Some matters are the preserve of the King alone. I pledge you my oath, I will help whenever it is in my power to do so. I cannot promise more."

Though he meant to reassure her, Midir's words only fed Gwen's fears. There *was* a secret plot against her, as Findabhair suspected. But what could it be? She cast a cold eye over the fairy hall. Was it a gilded cage? Or something worse? A mirage cloaking a hidden menace? Why did Finvarra want to ensnare her? Was there a worm at the heart of the shiny apple?

It was time to end the party. Time to get Findabhair. Time to go home.

At that very moment, on the other side of the Court, the King clapped his hands.

"Let the feasting commence!"

In the twinkling of an eye a great banquet table appeared, covered with snow-white linen. Stretching the length of the hall, it was laid out with dishes of gold and silver, and crystal goblets rimmed with gems. Though she had already been dazzled by every kind of wonder, Gwen could hardly believe what her eyes now beheld.

All things delicious and imaginable were spread out before her. The centerpiece was a whole roasted pig with a juicy red apple clenched in its jaw. Beside it stood a shellfish fantasia like a castle of coral dripping with sea flowers. There were chickens stuffed with raisins and chestnuts, nests of quails' eggs and prawns, roast duck with shallots, and mountains of pink lobster. Wheels of cheese were hemmed in by ham pies and beef pies and mince pies. Pyramids of fruit spilled into tiers of nuts, so that the soft ripe skins of grapes and cherries burst against the hard brown shells of filberts and walnuts. And oh, the side dishes! Pears dipped in melted cheddar. Crispy cucumber cups stuffed with crabmeat. And all sorts of mushrooms, for the fairy folk love mushrooms and none are poisonous to them. Chanterelles, morels, earthstars, and puffballs lay freshly picked in baskets or swimming in melted butter. Capped, frilled, scaled, gilled, speckled or plain, they were every color imaginable from purple, velvet black, bright red and orange to ivory white, pale yellow, gray-blue, and brown.

As for the desserts, Gwen's knees went weak at the sight of them. Strawberries smothered in cream and dusted with brown sugar. Raspberries coated in chocolate and frosted with white sugar. Brittle towers of honeycomb filled with gobs of ice cream and topped with swirled meringue. Stunning confections of marbled cake with layer upon layer upon layer of icing. There were gooseberry fools, cranberry and rhubarb jellies, melon jellies, green jellies of wild mint.

And a cold dark chocolate mousse that frothed like cream.

Inside Gwen, alarm bells were ringing. She knew she was facing her most perilous test. Did the King know that food was her weakness? The feast laid out was temptation itself.

At the head of the table Findabhair tried to catch her cousin's attention, but she couldn't move or call out. Beside her, Finvarra sat poised, ready to strike. His dark eyes narrowed. A faint smile played over his lips. A cat watching a mouse.

"Eat no food and drink no wine if you wish to return to your home again." Midir's whisper was urgent as he passed behind Gwen.

She groaned at the unfairness of the trial. All her favorite foods were there, sparkling with that extra touch of deliciousness that attends the forbidden. (Isn't this what happened to poor Adam and Eve?) The hot dishes wafted rich scents toward her. The cold dishes glinted and winked with enticement.

Gwen shuddered and then sighed.

"I'll have a bit of everything, please."

TWELVE

Gwen rushed to the table before she could change her mind. In a matter of seconds her plate was heaped high. A hush fell over the assembly. All eyes watched.

She savored her first bite.

Heaven. Ambrosia. Food of the gods.

The moment she swallowed, the company burst into riotous applause. Findabhair sank back, dismayed. The King leaped to his feet. His black cloak swirled behind him as he raised his arms in triumph. The silver star on his forehead blazed.

"The lady hath failed her trial! She is ours!"

The proclamation was met with a roar of approval, but it seemed the judgment was not unanimous. Ever mercurial and capricious in their humors, the fairy folk began to argue among themselves. As the feast got under way, voices of dissent were heard amid the revelry.

"She was the victor in the first test," Midir called out. "She tamed her night mare. Our claim is not pure."

Cheers and "Hear! Hear!" echoed from various quarters. Piqued by the challenge of one so high as the *Tánaiste*, those loyal to the King responded with catcalls. The bright lords and ladies were now seriously at odds.

Some cried "Unfair!" and "Poor sport, this!" while others, equally vehement, chanted "She is ours! She is ours!" Many were genuinely upset. Many more were convulsed with laughter. One portly red-cheeked fellow was holding his sides as if they might split with his guffaws. A twinkling sprite stood on her chair to make herself heard. A leprechaun removed one of his buckled shoes and began banging it on the table. Two pixies resorted to fisticuffs. The more serene of the elfin folk shook their golden locks and tapped cutlery against crystal to signal their annoyance.

As the company grew more agitated, their disharmony spilled over and into their surroundings. All the jellies began to quiver. Ice cubes rattled in the punch bowls. Dishes hopped on the table. Stoppers popped from the decanters of wine. When the chandeliers began to sway, a thousand candles flickered and spat. Thoroughly disgruntled by the whole affair, the roast pig stood up on its haunches, got down from the table, and marched out of the hall. Now the furniture began to twitch as if it, too, wished to depart. The very structure of the hall turned this way and that, shaken by the volatility of its occupants.

Pandemonium reigned.

Only two people seemed unaffected by the chaos: Findabhair, who was still trying to catch her cousin's attention, and Gwen herself, the cause of the controversy, eating away in a state of bliss.

Finvarra and Midir were now arguing vociferously, each backed by the shouts of their factions. Lightning crackled in the air around them. The center couldn't hold. Too much power and intensity was being unleashed. The great hall began to pitch and toss like a ship at sea. Everything went flying through the air—furniture, feast, and the fairies themselves.

The last thing Gwen remembered was the dish of chocolate mousse sailing past her. As she strained for a scoop she, too, was hurled upward.

Then she awoke.

On top of the Burren's Glen of Clab.

In the middle of the worst storm imaginable.

The night was black and raging. Rain poured in a relentless downfall. Wind and water lashed the hilltop. Whips of forked lightning streaked overhead, chased by deafening claps of thunder. It was as if the elemental hounds of hell had been loosed upon the land.

Reeling, Gwen struggled to her feet. She could barely see through the curtain of rain. The landscape was lost in gray sheets of water. The slope below her was a ragged shadow. Groping blindly, she began her descent. The dark rock was wet and slippery. She moved slowly, cautiously. Despite her care, she couldn't keep her footing. She started to slide down the scree in a shower of loose stones. There was nothing to grab on to. Her arms flailed in the air. As she gathered speed, she lost her balance and tumbled into a spill. She rolled uncontrollably, crying out with pain and fear. By the time she crashed to a halt at the bottom, she was cut and battered and dazed with shock.

Gwen lay on the ground, drenched and aching. Could her life get any worse? Weeping with sheer misery, she hauled herself up. She had to find shelter. *Where was she?* Nothing looked familiar in the dark. There were no streetlights or houses to show the way, only sodden fields and the ubiquitous stone walls that went on forever. Lowering her head against the wind and the rain, she picked a direction and trudged down the road. She needed to find the Quirkes. She had nowhere else to go.

Only when she spotted the sign for the *Fulacht Fia* did Gwen realize she had taken the wrong road. She was walking away from the Quirkes'! More tears joined the rainwater trickling down her face. She wanted to howl. Numb with defeat, she stared into the field where she had first met the fairies. If only Midir were there. But though there was no sign of her fairy champion, she spotted a bulky shape near the ring of pale stones. Her heart lifted. It was her knapsack, in the spot where she had left it when she mounted her horse!

With a cry of joy, she ran to retrieve her possessions. Zipping up her anorak, she felt instantly better. A little dryer, a little warmer, and her optimism returned. She had her bearings. She knew the way to the Quirke house from there.

Bundled up and with her hood pulled low, Gwen set out once more.

At last she spied the big house in the distance, a dark silhouette against the shadow of the mountain. But there were no warm yellow lights to hearten the traveler. With a pang of concern, she picked up her pace. As she turned a corner in the road, she was met by mayhem.

Cattle charged toward her, wild-eyed with panic. Beams of light shone from the car that crawled behind them. Running alongside the car were Katie and two younger girls, all in weatherproof macks. With shouts and long sticks, they struggled to herd the cattle.

Katie ran up to Gwen.

"Ho girl! This is no night to be out!"

Beneath the hood of her mack, Katie's face was aglow with excitement. She was obviously taking the storm in her stride.

"I don't suppose I could help?" Gwen offered half-heartedly.

"We're putting these lads with the others in the *Maher Buídhe*. They'll be more sheltered there, poor things. They want to hide under the trees, the most dangerous spot with the lightning. I don't think you could handle them, Gwen. They're pure wild with fright. Go up to the house. The electricity's knocked off, but there's a fire in the grate. If you'd like to help, make us something hot for when we get back."

"I will," Gwen promised.

Katie gave her a hard look, and was about to say something when thunder pealed overhead. The cows bellowed in terror and bolted down the road. Katie raced after them.

When Gwen reached the house, she found it blacked out except for the living room where the hearth fire was lit. The thatched roof was raining in spots. Buckets and pots had been set out to catch the drips. In the kitchen, more basins plonked to the tune of falling water. A big Stanley range heated the room, with a black kettle simmering on the hob. There was a wooden dresser stacked with blue china and a painting of the Sacred Heart on the wall. Under the table, the dog cowered from the thunder like a frightened child.

"It's okay, Bran," she said soothingly, but he stared back at her with the dumb terror of beasts.

Gwen dried herself and changed her clothes. She was shocked by the number of cuts and bruises she had, but nothing looked serious. Rummaging around the kitchen, she tried to keep busy. She needed to do something, anything, to keep her mind off her disastrous visit to Faerie. Homemade soup would be good. Chopping carrots, celery, onions, and potatoes, she added them to a chicken stock with handfuls of barley. Then she sliced bread for ham and cheese sandwiches. When the soup began to bubble, the homely smell of simple fare was a damning reminder. Only a short while ago she had gorged herself on food far richer. Her stomach felt queasy, as if she had devoured a whole box of chocolates in one go.

She pushed the memory away. Instead, she thought of the Quirke women out battling the elements.

When the sandwiches were ready, she set the table in the living room. The hearth fire was dying down, so she added more turf. Then she found candles to place in saucers around the room. Having done all she could, she sank into a big chair and dozed fitfully.

The evening's events were taking their toll. She felt drained and feverish. The candlelight confused her, harking back to the fairy hall. Outside the window, the Burren mountains were blue-black and shining, like whales sailing through a storm-driven sea. The wind howled above the house like the wails of a banshee. Everything seemed formless and chaotic.

Only when she heard the sound of a car in the driveway was she able to rouse herself to put out the food.

The Quirkes bustled into the house, shaking out wet macks and pulling off boots. Their worn faces brightened at the scene before them. Bowls of piping-hot soup had been set on the table, with plates of sandwiches and a big pot of tea.

Katie introduced Gwen to her mother and sisters.

"The fire blazing and all," Mrs. Quirke said warmly. "You're a most welcome guest, my dear."

While the family enjoyed their supper, Gwen sipped a cup of weak tea.

"Not eating?" Katie asked, with a deliberate stare.

Gwen looked away.

"I've had too much tonight already."

The older girl frowned but said nothing, while the others chatted around the table.

"I've seen many a bad storm in my day," Mrs. Quirke stated, "but this beats all. You brought the bad weather, Gwen."

Though she knew it was a figure of speech, Gwen winced. Not for the first time that night she wondered if the storm was fairy fury. *Did* she cause it?

It was later, when the spare bed was made up in Katie's room and Gwen was almost asleep, that the other girl questioned her. Katie's face looked grave in the candlelight.

"I don't want to offend you, Gwen, and maybe it's none of my business, but I'm going to ask you anyway. Are you on something? Were you meeting a drug pusher tonight?"

A strange lassitude had overcome Gwen. Her thoughts were soft and white like puffs of cotton wool. Had Katie asked for her name, she would have hesitated. But the question was more serious, though utterly absurd. While one part of Gwen wanted to laugh, she also felt like crying. Katie was acting like a big sister. She obviously cared about Gwen.

"They don't deal in drugs," Gwen answered slowly. "They deal in dreams. Maybe it has the same effect?"

Katie was about to demand an explanation, when Gwen ended their talk by falling asleep.

Thirteen

The next morning Gwen woke to find Katie in a chair by her bedside.

"This must be what a hangover feels like," Gwen groaned.

Her throat was parched, she felt hot and achy, and her head throbbed as if it housed an orchestra of hammers and tongs.

"You mean you don't know?" the older girl asked. Her look of concern changed to a grin.

"Nope. I've never taken drugs, to answer your question, and that includes alcohol. Boy, do I feel awful."

Gwen sat up shakily.

"You had a rough night," her friend said quietly. "Fever and bad dreams. Mam said to call the doctor if you didn't improve today. I'm really ashamed of myself. You were acting so odd, but it didn't occur to me that you might be coming down with something. I'm a right *amadán*."

"I don't know what that is but I'm sure you're not." Gwen managed to smile. "And your suspicions weren't totally wrong. Something *is* going on, but not what you thought."

A silence fell between them, resonant with unspoken questions and answers. It was obvious that Katie sensed some mystery afoot but didn't want to burden Gwen with her curiosity. Gwen, in turn, was debating on how much she would or could say. After the fiasco at the fairy banquet, she badly needed advice. She had no idea what to do next.

"I'm going to ask you something, Katie," she said tentatively. It was a hunch but she was thinking of Mattie, and also of Katie's red hair. "It'll sound crazy, but I'm not joking. Okay?"

"You're on," said Katie. "I'm all ears."

"Do you believe in fairies?"

Katie's eyes widened but to Gwen's relief she didn't laugh, nor did she look scornful.

"Yes," she said simply. "Ever since I was a little girl. I still leave a saucer of cream or milk on the windowsill at night, or some wine if we have it for dinner. It's an old tradition, a courtesy. The family thinks I'm daft, but I do it anyway."

"Have you ever seen them?"

"No, but things happen. I've never told a soul." She lowered her voice. "The Good People don't like being talked about."

"What kind of things?" Gwen whispered.

"Ach, well, you could put it down to fancy or coincidence. Little things. Sometimes breaches in the walls are mended overnight. And once I couldn't find a ewe, and her with a lamb inside her. I was worried sick. Searched everywhere. It was nearly dark, and I was almost at the top of Slievecarron and still no sign of her, when I heard the music. A sweet piping sound, high up in the air. It seemed to beckon to me, so I followed after it. It led me right to her, where she lay caught in barbed wire. Maybe it's all in the head, but I believe they look out for me."

"You're the kind of person they would help."

"How would you know that?"

A hush fell over them. Both had reached the point where secrets could be aired without fear of judgment.

Gwen told her story to date, leaving out nothing. After describing the calamity at the banquet, she finished dismally.

"I've screwed everything up. I haven't a clue how to get back, but I've got to reach Findabhair. There's something wrong with Faerie. She knows it herself. Something creepy hiding in the dark. I've got to get her out of there before it's too late. Before something bad happens."

Katie was listening in stunned silence. She rummaged in her pockets to find a cigarette.

"Sorry for polluting your air, but I can't manage this without a smoke. I can hardly get my head around it!"

Gwen got out of bed and dressed herself, but she was moving slowly. She felt weak and dizzy.

"I'll make you a big fry for your breakfast," Katie offered.

"Ugh, no. The thought of food makes me ill. And that's not right!"

"Shouldn't you rest then?"

"There's no time. I must get after them. They're probably doing this to hold me back, but it won't work."

"That's the spirit!" said Katie. "What'll we do? Where shall we go?"

Gwen noted the "we" gratefully. Despite her brave words she was wondering if she had the strength to do anything.

"Back to the Ancient Eating Place. Midir met me there before. He's my best bet in a crunch."

"We'll take the motorbike."

"Don't you have work to do?" Gwen said guiltily. "I shouldn't be dragging you into this."

"Mam and the girls are at it. I'm supposed to be looking after you and that's what I'm doing, right?"

As they sped down the road, Gwen was revived by the cool rush of air. The Burren looked worn and bedraggled after the storm. The road was littered with branches and twigs. The limestone pavements glistened with rainfall. A turlough had risen to flood a field.

When they reached the *Fulacht Fia*, their hopes were quashed. The site was empty, nothing but wet grass and sodden ground. A cold wind blew over the ring of stones.

"He promised to help."

Disappointed, Gwen sat down wearily on a rock.

Undaunted, Katie continued to scout the area until she, too, gave up and joined her friend.

"This is hopeless," sighed Gwen. "How to find a fairy in a haystack?"

"*Ssh,*" said Katie suddenly. "Do you hear something?"

Both were suddenly still and alert. The sounds came from behind them. Slowly they turned to face the clump of bushes a short distance away. Nothing could be seen through the dense tangle of hazel, but the noises came from the other side. A low crunching and munching, accompanied by little sighs and snorts.

Katie let out a low laugh. She was about to stand up to see whose goats had strayed, when the voices began. Gwen grabbed her arm and they both sat frozen, hardly daring to breathe.

"She made a right hames of the feast last night."

"Bejapers and she did. Ruptions and ructions to beat the band. The place nearly burst asunder."

"There'll be talk of it for ages to come."

"That's what they get for letting the likes of them into the manor house."

"Asha, they're not all bad. What about our Katie?"

"Our good neighbor?"

"The best there is."

"She's a friend of your one, you know."

"She is that."

"I'm sure she'd want us to lend a hand and all."

"Oh aye. And we'd have the wrath of the Boss down about our ears before you could say 'taw shay mahogany gaspipes.'"

"He'd leave us as we are for another hundred years."

"Ah now, he'd get over it."

"He wouldn't."

"He would."

"He wouldn't."

"He would."

"And he would not."

"Well, who then is going to tell the *girseach* that the Court has upped and gone to Boyle?"

"Boyle in the County of Roscommon?"

"Aye."

"Sure who would tell her that?"

"Not me."

"Me neither."

"But she might overhear us and if she did, I'm thinking, bedad, it wouldn't be our fault now would it?"

"Not at'all. Not at'all. We couldn't be held accountable if them ones takes to eavesdropping."

"Right you are then."

"And that's that."

The voices fell silent.

Katie uttered a little cry and made a dash for her bike, with Gwen close behind. Engine roaring, they sped away. Only when she had put some distance between herself and the Eating Place did Katie stop to look back. Behind the bushes, a herd of feral goats were grazing. With their scraggly beards, crescent-shaped horns, and shaggy coats they looked like old wizards crawling about on all fours. One raised its head to stare at her fixedly.

"Lord God above," Katie swore softly.

She was gripping the handlebars so hard her knuckles were white.

Gwen understood.

"Scary, isn't it?"

The first encounter was always a deep shock.

When they reached the farmhouse, Katie was still too shaken to talk. Sinking into the sofa, she stared into space.

Gwen brought her a cup of tea, then went to pack. Consulting her map, she found the town of Boyle in County Roscommon, though at first she had been look-ing for a place called "Boil." When she returned to the living room, her friend was at the window, gazing over the mountains.

"I'm off, Katie. I'm sure you know why. Thanks so much for everything. Especially this. You heard what they said. If it wasn't for you they wouldn't have helped me."

"No, no. Thank *you*, Gwen!"

Katie's eyes shone with a startling light. Now that her initial terror had subsided, in its wake brimmed an irre-pressible awe and delight.

Gwen saw how she herself must have appeared to Mattie and decided that "touched" didn't look so bad after all.

"You can't know what this means to me." Katie's voice shook. "To know that they are really and truly here. Sometimes I wonder why I bother to keep going. There's so much work to do and never enough hands to do it. You build a wall, it falls down. You tend your cattle day in and day out, then one of them contracts TB and you can't sell any. You sit up all night with a sick lamb and she dies in the morning. And now there's the threat of mad cow disease as well. This year's been the worst of all, with Da in the hospital and us not knowing if he'll get well."

"Oh Katie," Gwen said. "I'm so sorry."

Only now did she realize how hard her friend's life was.

Katie waved away the sympathy and held her head proudly. "That's farming. Nobody said it would be easy. I love it and I wouldn't want to do anything else. But sometimes you need something to keep you going. A dream, or a vision of the future maybe. The fairies have always been my consolation." Katie looked out the window. "And they called me their good neighbor!"

"They know a good thing when they see it." Gwen smiled.

"I want to come with you."

"No way. I've already got one to haul out of Faerie. I'm not going for two."

Katie looked crestfallen, but Gwen's words made sense.

"You're right. I'd never come back. But promise me this. I said it before and I'll say it again—if you ever need help you're to call on me, right?" Katie pretended to spit on her hand and then held it out. "Make it a deal, like a true farmer."

Laughing, Gwen mimicked her actions and they shook on the agreement.

"I'll drive you to the main road. Do you know where you're going?"

"Not really. But that hasn't stopped me yet."

Fourteen

"Here you are now, love. Boyle."

The truck driver pulled up the long vehicle on a narrow street. The air brakes hissed like a snake.

Gwen surfaced with a jolt.

"Sorry, what did you say?"

It had happened again! One minute she was sitting there, looking out the window. The next, she was in a forest with shafts of sunlight falling around her and voices calling through the air.

"It's Boyle you want, isn't it?" said the driver.

"Oh. Yes. Thank you."

Gwen climbed down from the high cab, and wandered aimlessly through the town. The streets followed the hilly contours of the landscape. Houses, shops, and pubs creeped up and down the road. When she came to a stone bridge, she stopped to gaze at the river below. Long stems of green starwort streamed under the water. Mesmerized, she watched as they were tugged and swayed by the flow of the current.

What was she doing here?

The day had been a blur of faces and places. She had barely managed to keep on track. Images from the banquet hall kept flashing through her mind, along with giddy colors and leering features. Sometimes her ears throbbed with music, or the raucous sounds of revelry. Worse was the sudden shift of scene, when she found herself somewhere else entirely. A green meadow filled with light, or that early morning forest. She would have been worried, but for the vagueness that muffled her. Like a leaf drifting downstream, she felt drawn inexorably by some invisible force.

On the outskirts of Boyle, Gwen came upon the ruins of a medieval monastery. As if lost in a dream, she entered through the gatehouse and rambled around. The site was grand and airy with arches spanning rows of stone pillars and fluted columns. High lancet windows looked out on leafy trees. Overhead shone the blue canopy of sky. The graveled cloister walk trimmed a wide square of lawn. To her left a great vaulted aisle led to the church tower, transept, and presbytery. The altars were in the east, to face the rising sun. Ahead and to her right were the remnants of the chapter house, infirmary, book room, kitchens, refectory, and dormitories.

Gwen shielded her eyes against the glare of sunlit stone. Why was she here? Church bells pealed in the distance. She felt sleepy, and her sight began to waver. For a brief frightening moment she saw ghostly figures pad past her. They were monks in long habits, with their arms tucked into their sleeves and heads bowed in prayer.

She looked back through the gatehouse at the silhouette of Boyle. The town was veiled as if by heat waves. The brick buildings kept fading in and out, to be replaced by huts of wattle and daub. Carts pulled by donkeys moved through the traffic, while people in rough homespun mingled with the present-day crowds.

"What's happening to me?"

Even the question wavered in her mind. She felt like a ghost herself, pale and insubstantial. Not quite there, not quite anywhere. The languor was difficult to fight, being strangely pleasant. Like the gentle persistence of much-needed sleep, it nudged her to surrender. She sat down beneath a yew tree at the heart of the cloister. Though she couldn't recall seeing it when she first entered, the tree welcomed her into its shady embrace. The red bark was cool at her back, the scent of leaves was soothing, and the hum of bees in the warm foliage was like a lullaby. She was glad to be out of the sun. It was a good spot for a nap. Closing her eyes, she slumped into a doze.

Only to be roughly shaken awake.

"Get thee hence, maiden!" the young monk urged. "If one of the *Manaigh Liath* even touches thee, thou wilt be trapped in this time!"

"What?"

She was up in an instant. The warning was enough to galvanize her, but the shock of what she saw took a moment to sink in. Parts of the monastery were fully restored. The wooden beams of a slate-shingled roof covered nave and aisle. A choir of male voices echoed from the church. The scent of frankincense wafted from the chancel. The rest of the buildings were still in ruins. Gwen's heart skipped a beat as she grasped the situation. Like a titanic ship sinking into the ocean, the monastery was slipping back through time. If she didn't escape, she would slip back with it!

Now the abbot himself stepped out of the rectory and spied her. He started to shout and gesticulate.

From every quarter Gray Monks came running. They, too, were shouting and pointing at her. Terrified, Gwen looked for an exit. The gatehouse was halfway into the past. A group of monks stood near it. She ran instead to a large walled area that was still in her own time. Used for storing broken pieces of stone—arches, cornices, tombstones, and baptismal fonts—it was like a hall of bleached bones. She crouched behind a slab of granite. *What to do? What to do?*

She didn't want to be trapped in the past! Living out her life in the wrong time and place. Though she didn't know much about the Middle Ages, she suspected it wasn't the best time to be female. Getting caught in a monastery could only make matters worse. She'd be in terrible trouble. What if they put her in prison? Would she be flogged? Wasn't this the time they burned women as witches?

The dark thoughts scurried through her mind like rats, even as warning bells tolled throughout the cloister.

Everywhere she looked, monks were scouring the buildings, searching for her. A few ran past, but they couldn't see her. Not yet. But it wouldn't be long before they did. The past was seeping closer, like waves lapping at the shore. Soon the tide would come in. Soon it would drown her.

Gwen kept an anguished watch on the gatehouse. Only a portion was left in the present. Barely enough for her to squeeze through. She would have to move soon before it was too late.

There was a moment when her will failed her. She dreaded leaving the safety of her hiding place. Her legs went weak. *I can't do it, I can't.* Then something caught her eye. A shattered tombstone. It had originally been engraved with a full-length figure but only a small piece remained, a section of torso along with the head. Though the relief was worn down, it was still discernible. A woman with curly hair like snakes. Medusa? Peering closer, Gwen's blood ran cold. The carved face was a mirror of her own! She suddenly knew. If she didn't go now she would die there, far away in the past.

Terror spurred her on.

So, too, the clamor that erupted as soon as she ran across the cloister. The gatehouse seemed miles away. Could she make it? She was no athlete and hardly fit. They were closing in on her. She could hear the thump of sandaled feet and the rasp of coarse breaths around her. She was almost there. She had reached the gatehouse. Only a few steps . . .

No!

The monk lurking in the shadows stepped out to confront her. He was like the Grim Reaper with his face lost in a gray cowl. Her heart sank. The others were shouting at him to grab her. She didn't stop. Feinting to the right to throw him off guard, she made a dash to the left. It almost worked. But he recovered too fast. His hand shot out. She yelled as he gripped her. Despite her kicks and screams, he held on tight.

Then he hauled her through the gatehouse, across the threshold of the monastery.

As soon as they passed through the gates, the noise of pursuit ended. It was as if a door had slammed shut behind them. Now the monk released her. In their scuffle, his hood had fallen back. Sunlight glinted on the red-gold hair.

"Midir!"

Gasping with relief, she almost wept as she thanked him.

"Do not tarry here," he said quickly, "lest the portal open again. Flee from this place, as far as you can."

There was no need for urging. Though Boyle Abbey was an empty ruin once more, the air around it shimmered with menace. But she didn't run away.

"Where's Findabhair?" she demanded. "I've got to see her!"

Midir hesitated a moment.

"Can you not leave her to her fate?"

Gwen had barely caught her breath, now her heart beat wildly.

"What do you mean?"

A veiled look fell over Midir's features, the same expression he had worn in the fairy hall when he spoke of the King's schemes. His tone was evasive.

"It is either you or her, I see that now, and I would not have you harmed."

Gwen felt the chill of foreboding. His words were ominous. She tried to question him further, but he refused to say more. She sensed the dark side of Faerie behind his silence.

"You promised to help me," she reminded him. "If you know where she is, please tell me."

"You will not turn from this path, despite my plea?"

"Not without her," Gwen insisted.

"So be it," he sighed. "Go into the town, to the House of the Little Branch. You will see the sign."

She hurried away, shaken to the core. Things were getting worse. Finvarra had upped the stakes. If it weren't for Gwen's champion in the other world, who knew what had awaited her, trapped in the past? The King was playing a dangerous game. Might it prove fatal? With a shudder, she remembered her cousin's words.

They can get away with murder without batting an eyelid.
And then there were Midir's. *It is either you or her, I see
that now, and I would not have you harmed.*

It was more important than ever that she reach
Findabhair.

"The House of the Little Branch," she repeated to herself, as she searched Boyle for anything resembling Midir's
instructions. "Doesn't sound like a place in modern
Ireland. And how will I recognize the sign he mentioned?"

At the top of the town, past the clock tower, Gwen
found what she was looking for. An antique placard
creaked gently in the breeze, over the door of a pub. *An
Craoibhín*. Though she couldn't translate the name, the
picture was enough to convince her. It showed the branch
of an oak tree dangling with mistletoe.

"It's a public 'house' and he meant a real sign. Here I'm
expecting something mystical. Will I ever figure these guys
out?"

As the pub door swung open, she was greeted by a blast
of music. A *seisiún* was in progress and the place was
packed. Tourists and local people sat together at tables
laden with whiskey and porter. In a half circle near the bar,
as if onstage, were musicians playing traditional music.

Their virtuosity was dazzling. In a tumult of merry
reels, jigs, and hornpipes, tune chased after tune without
stopping for breath. The tin whistle trilled like birds scattered in flight. The *bodhrán* drum rumbled like peals of
thunder. The elbow pipes were a skirl of sound, as if a hive

of bees sang in tenor and bass. But it was the fiddler who was the most thrilling of all. His bow skipped over taut strings, a dancer leaping! As his listeners tried to follow the wild notes, he whipped them along at a frenzied pace—up mountains, down glens, and across rushing rivers—till they jiggled and jittered like puppets on a string.

When the madcap music ended with a flourish, they roared for more. Never had they heard the like!

Now the musicians started up a slow sweet air. The singer cleared her throat, and rested her hand on the knee of the fiddle-player.

A gypsy rover came o'er the hill,
And down to the valley so shady,
He whistled and he sang,
Till the green woods rang,
And he won the heart of a la-a-a-dy.

Gwen struggled to get a grip on reality. Still reeling from her close escape at the monastery, she could hardly take in this cozy tableau. In jeans and T-shirts the musicians looked like any other group of young people, albeit extremely beautiful. Everyone in the pub accepted them as normal while wonderfully gifted. But Gwen knew the truth. There was only one human to be found among them.

For that was Findabhair blithely singing away, her hand on the denimed knee of the King of Faerie!

She left her home to seek her fate,
And roam the land all over,
For her kin she didn't wait,
But followed the gypsy rover.

Gwen tried to approach the group, but couldn't get near. A wall of bodies, as impenetrable as a rampart, barred her way. A young couple made room for her on a bench against the wall. She sat down, keeping her eyes on her cousin. Why was Findabhair acting as if she didn't see her? She must have spotted Gwen coming into the pub. What was going on? And she was singing the ballad with surprising emotion for someone who always said she hated folk music.

Gwen straightened up. Was it a signal? Was Findabhair trying to tell her something?

You'll find us there without a care
At the heart of the woods of Sheegar-ar-ar-a.

The fiddler, who was Finvarra, suddenly raised his hand. The music screeched to a halt. With a sardonic glance at Findabhair, he declared the session over. Despite cries of dismay and calls for more, the musicians packed up their gear in a whirlwind of motion and exited the pub.

The audience sat stunned. They didn't know what had hit them. The publican collapsed in a chair, mopping his brow. He rarely got a crowd at suppertime and had been caught off guard without his barman.

"The Irish are strange, *non?*" said a French tourist to Gwen.

"*Oui,*" she agreed. "But you gotta love them anyway."

Unlike the others, Gwen wasn't disturbed by the band's departure. She had picked up her cousin's message loud and clear. Now all she had to do was find "Sheegara."

Fifteen

L ooking for a tourist office, Gwen was directed to another pub in the town. It was dimly lit and cozy, with dark wooden furniture and a small fire in the grate. None of the scenic maps or pamphlets on display made any reference to a place called Sheegara. The proprietor behind the bar had never heard of it, nor had his wife who was working in the kitchen. The customers who sat drinking or reading their newspapers also shook their heads.

Gwen was beginning to wonder if she had heard Findabhair right, when an old man in the corner piped up querulously.

"Sure none of ye would know the old place names anymore. They're all dead and buried with the rest of old Ireland. Gone with the black bicycles that used to lean against the hedgerows. Gone with the dancing at the crossroads and the bottled porter."

"Never mind the sermon, Bernie," the publican said.

"Tell the girl where it is, if you know, and I'm sure that you do." He winked at Gwen. "If it's local history you want, he's your man."

Bernie scowled at the publican and hunched over his drink. It was evident that he would say no more. But there was too much at stake for Gwen to give up easily. She saw that the old man was drinking Guinness, and she ordered a bottle and brought it over to him.

Bernie wore the dark suit favored by Irish farmers, with his trousers tucked into wellington boots. His hands were gnarled, the fingers yellowed by tobacco stains. Watery eyes peered out from a face lined like a dried riverbed. When he spied the drink, he pushed back his cap and nodded to her.

Gwen sat down.

"Sheegara," he said, with maddening slowness. His hand shook a little as he poured the black stout into the glass. Bubbles frothed to the rim. "It's the anglified pronouncement for the townland of *Sídhe Gáire*, meaning 'the laughing fairies.'"

"Can you tell me where it is?" she asked eagerly.

"I can. Go out the town apace, past the old abbey, and on up the Sligo Road. Take the first turn to your right and you're heading straight for it. Where is it in the townland you might be going?"

"A forest or wood?"

The old man took a long gulp of his drink. His Adam's apple bobbed up and down as he swallowed. When he slammed the glass back onto the table, Gwen jumped.

"There's new trees up there planted by the Forestry and making a ruination of the land. Is it them you're after?"

"I don't know," she said uncertainly, "I don't think so. Are there other woods?"

"There be old ones that are a thing of beauty, a home for wild creatures, and a joy to walk in. Then there be new ones grown for money in thin straight lines, ready for the chop. It's blood money, I tell ye, that turns good pasture into a wasteland."

"I'm sure they wouldn't approve of that," she said. "Definitely an old one."

The barman had come over to wipe the table. He threw Gwen an odd look, but Bernie was now regarding her as a kindred soul and smiled benevolently.

"Long before your time, girleen, there was talk of an ancient grove up there. The Forest of the Red Fairies it was called, and they say it was an enchanted place. You'd want to put your best foot forward if you're looking for it. It'd be twilight before ye find it, I'm thinking."

"The right time for the right place," she murmured.

She stood up to leave, thanking the old man profusely. His eyes twinkled.

"Good luck and God bless."

As Gwen left the town, following Bernie's directions, she wondered briefly if his gray hair had been red when he was young.

Ahead of her rose the ruined walls of Boyle Abbey.

Shuddering at the sight, she hurried past. Once she reached the Sligo Road, her step grew more confident. She congratulated herself. Despite their tricks, she was still hot on the heels of the fairy court. Nancy Drew and the Case of the Missing Fairies.

Her good humor helped to offset the fact that she felt physically weak and sometimes groggy. She hadn't eaten a meal since the fairy banquet. The idea of food was revolting. Somewhere in the back of her mind this worried her, but she told herself she had a stomach bug.

Though the Sligo road was busy with traffic, she decided not to hitchhike. She didn't want to miss the turn that Bernie had mentioned. It wasn't long before she reached it. Soon she found herself walking a lonely byway into the hills. There were no houses or cars in sight. The lane twisted and turned like a snake in the grass. Dense hedgerows of hawthorn shaded her path. Fields of purple heather rolled away below her. Slowly a breathtaking view unfurled: a silver chain of lakes at the throat of blue mountains.

Except for the occasional sheep or cattle, Gwen was utterly alone. At one point she passed a little cottage half-buried in a ditch. The once whitewashed walls were gray with neglect. Tattered lace curtains hung limp and dusty. A vase of dead flowers stood in the front window. She sensed some meaning to the place, but she wasn't sure what. The old man's words echoed through her mind. *Gone with the rest of old Ireland.* How much had been lost? And why?

Though there were no signposts she sensed she was in

the right place, even as she had known it in the Burren. The fairies seemed to favor forsaken regions. Were they a beleaguered race holding out in the last patches of countryside? Would the spread of towns eventually push them out altogether? Were they doomed, like so many other wild creatures, before the onslaught of man?

A strange melancholy settled over her. She felt bowed down, as if a heavy mantle had settled on her shoulders. The evening breeze was now a wind that cried desolately over the fields.

Ochón! Ochón ó!

She could barely put one foot in front of the other. Why was she so burdened with grief? Whose feelings were these? With relief, she spotted a figure on the road ahead. Though her feet felt leaden she forced herself onward, anxious to meet another soul.

The old woman stood in the shadow of the hedgerow, leaning on a blackthorn stick. She was small and stooped. A dark shawl draped her head and shoulders, with wisps of gray hair trailing out like smoke. The hem of her skirt fell to heavy laced boots caked with mud. Her face was brown and crumpled but it was her eyes that caught Gwen, two black beads bright with laughter.

"*Nach breá an tráthnóna é, a chailín,*" she said in Irish. When Gwen stared at her blankly, she spoke again. "Isn't it a fine evening, my girl?"

Happy to have company, Gwen stopped to chat. After pleasantries about the weather, she asked for directions to Sheegara.

"Oh aye. You be in the realm of *Sídhe Gáire*. The laughing fairies are just beyant. This sweet road and your two fine feet will soon take you there."

"Thank you," said Gwen.

She was reluctant to leave. There was something about the old woman that fascinated her. Was she a fairy? Or was she like the others Gwen had met in her travels, those Irish in tune with a different world? The mingling of the races was complex and puzzling. How could she know for certain who belonged to which?

"Will ye bide here with me awhile?" the old woman pleaded. "I've no one about me these long days. They've all left for the town or Amerikay."

Gwen knew what it was like to be left behind. She felt sorry for her. The evening had turned soft and hazy. A slow sunset was suffusing the sky. The clouds glowed burnt orange and red. The necklace of lakes reflected the sky's colors like glimmering gems. Brooding over them, the Curlew Mountains were awash with pale purple.

The old woman began to speak in a singsong voice that rose and fell with the wind.

"*I have seen a land where summer dwells, a faraway country. There stands a fair bright wood of branching oak, full of red sap, where sweet birds nest. At eventide cools the sun-steeped earth in a shower of dew, like dark drops of honey. Acorns fall from the trees and into a stream, foam-flecked and murmuring.*"

Gwen felt her limbs relax. What was the hurry? Where was she going? Why not stay and enjoy the scenery and listen to the story the old woman was telling? Time enough to chase after phantoms and fairies. Here was true beauty spread at her feet, like embroidered cloths. Why not stay and enjoy it?

"In that most delightful country, they dwell in palaces of precious stones and radiant summer houses surrounded by lemon trees. See you now the little hostel thatched with bird wings? Inside is a table set with dishes of blue crystal. There sits a slender woman, perfect as a pearl, playing the harp. She wears a gown of dark-green satin and a mantle fringed with gold."

A drowsy feeling came over Gwen. The jeweled words hovered in the air like hummingbirds. Her eyelids grew heavy and fluttered closed. She didn't see the changes overtaking the old woman. How the creased face grew longer, the small body thinner. Nor did Gwen notice the briars that reached out from the hedgerow to clutch at her legs. With each gust of wind, the tendrils moved closer, clinging to her clothes and twining like ivy. Only when the brambles crawled up her arms did the prick of a thorn break the spell. With horror, Gwen saw that she was bound fast.

Trapped again! And so quickly! She had been caught unawares, not expecting another attempt so soon. Hadn't Findabhair warned her not to underestimate the King? *He's a tricky divil.* Furious at herself as well as the fairies, Gwen struggled against her bonds.

The moment she moved, the brambles tightened their grip. Tiny barbs pricked her like pins and needles. She cried out in pain. The threat was clear. *If you fight us, it will get worse.* The briars continued to weave their web, enclosing her in a dark cocoon. The green smell of vegetation was thick and suffocating. The world outside began to fade.

A cold whisper shivered through the leafage.

You are the Hunted and the Sacrifice.

"Let go of me!" she screamed in terror, looking for the old woman.

But the decoy herself had been drawn into the hedge. The wrinkled brown skin was the knotted bark of branches. The skirt and shawl were a mass of leaves. The black beady eyes were two ripened berries.

Gwen was shouting at a bush.

That was the last straw. Her fury exploded and overcame her fear. With their pranks and their magic, the fairies were literally driving her insane.

"That's it! I've had it!" she roared again.

Now she wrestled the hawthorn with the strength of rage. Leaves flew in the air. Brambles cracked as she elbowed them back. Though the thorns bit and scratched, she flailed and clawed till her arms were clear, and then her legs. Once she could kick, the fight was won. With a yell of triumph, she stomped her way out.

Free at last, she ran up the road.

But though she had won the battle, Gwen had paid a price. As she raced away, her sight blurred with tears. She was scratched and bleeding, and her clothes were torn. The hedge had also taken her knapsack. And what of the threat it had whispered to her? Were they hoping to scare her away, so she would give up on Findabhair?

"Not likely," she muttered.

She was angry now. No more Ms. Nice Guy. It was time to fight back.

Sixteen

S he didn't stop running till the road itself came to an
end. In front of her was a wooden gate locked with a
chain. Beyond it ranged a plantation of young pine. The
rows of trees stood to attention, just as Bernie had
described, like soldiers about to be hewn down. Gwen did-
n't think twice, but climbed over the gate and plunged into
the forest. Evening was closing fast. Dusk muted the sky.
Somewhere inside this new growth was the ancient wood
of Sheegara, and she had to find it before darkness fell.

The scent of pine sharpened the air. Dried needles and
cones crunched underfoot. Some of the trees were so thin
they leaned against each other like wounded comrades.
Always new and never allowed to mature, they couldn't
nourish a healthy understory. The earth was gashed from
successive cuttings, and worn out from overwork. A weari-
ness hung in the air. No birds sang. Gwen felt oppressed by
the silence. She knew she wouldn't find fairies here.

Further she went, seeking the heart of the woods. Her

steps began to falter. The thrust of her anger was petering away into the deepening shadows. This forest wasn't friendly. Did it harbor danger? The dark thing of Faerie that seemed to haunt her? Her thoughts turned to Little Red Riding Hood and ravening wolves. She picked up her pace, glancing about nervously.

At last the man-made lines of trees gave way to a natural disorder and beauty. The delicate greens of birch and willow mingled with white poplar and the old gold of oak. A silvery green lichen frosted branch and twig. The ground was springy with a mat of moss. As the sky darkened and the pale moon came out, threads of light quivered through the forest. Gwen tread with lighter steps. This wood instilled peace. Though night was falling like a starry cloak, she wasn't afraid. They were near, she could sense them.

Then she heard the music. High notes piping like a silver flute. Dancing in the air. Tempting and teasing. They beckoned to her.

Her pulse raced. Excitement pressed against her till she could hardly breathe. She crept through the underbrush. Ahead shone a fiery light, as if the sun had set in the forest and was burning there. Closer she drew, crouching in the greenery. As she peeped out from the shelter of the leaves, her eyes grew big. For only now, when she saw them again, did Gwen admit that she had been longing for them.

There in a moonlit forest glade, around a bright bonfire, danced the fairies. Flickering and flitting like flames themselves, they footed with unruly glee. Whirling dervishes and spinning tops would be slow beside them. They capered in giddy circles like eddies of wind.

She couldn't tell if they were tall or tiny. Their clothes were flower petals and puffs of thistledown, yet their limbs seemed longer than the trunks of the trees. Holly and mistletoe circled their wrists like red-and-white bracelets. Berries dangled from their ears, bluebells crowned their hair. Where they had been silver against the Burren's gray stone, here they were of darker coloring—russet-brown, midnight-black, dark-green, and ruddy. Were they chameleons? Camouflaged by their surroundings? Was their glamour in the fairy hall but another guise? Truly they were wildish things, not of humanity, but nature's children.

Gwen watched them, enthralled.

Suddenly a dark form leaped over the bonfire, scattering the fairies with the shriek of a hawk. Vivid colors gleamed on his body like metallic paint. His dark eyes were scrolled with kohl. His long black hair was sleek and glossy. In command of the clearing, he began to dance. It was a breathtaking display of grace and control. At first he stepped slowly, as if in a dream, then he switched to quick startling motions. The tilt of his head or the crook of his arm. Even his eyes flitted and flicked. And his fingers and toes. Each exquisite movement was an intensity of passion honed to perfection—the first shoot of a leaf, a bird breaking its shell, a dragonfly struggling to unveil its wings. In every part of his being, he was dance itself. On his brow glittered the sovereign star. Finvarra, the King, Lord of the Dance.

"Isn't he beautiful?"

The husky whisper took Gwen by surprise. She almost stumbled from her hiding place. Her face flushed hot in the cool night air.

"Don't speak," warned Findabhair.

She grasped Gwen's arm and led her through the forest. They came to the ruins of an old stone wall that once enclosed an apple orchard. The apple trees had long since run wild and were overgrown with tangles of elder and ivy. The two followed the wall till they reached a stream that glimmered in the moonlight like quicksilver. Findabhair sat on the bank and dangled her feet in the water. She motioned to Gwen to join her, but the other hung back.

Gwen was stunned by her cousin's appearance. Findabhair's clothes were shredded in ribbons and interlaced with wildflowers. Her feet and arms were bare, her skin nut-brown. A daisy chain wreathed her long thick hair. The golden curls stood out like a bush, matted with leaves. She was beautiful in a fierce wild way, but the eyes were too bright, too wild.

Oblivious to Gwen's dismay, Findabhair spoke blithely.

"We can talk here. Water affects their powers. Am I ever glad to see you! I've been mad with worry. You're in terrible trouble. How are you feeling?"

"Never mind that!" Gwen urged. "Let's go! This is your chance to escape!"

The peal of laughter was like a blow.

"Why would I need to escape? I'm not a prisoner."

Gwen was dumbstruck. Was this really her cousin? Or was she under a spell?

Findabhair stopped laughing. Now her look was grave. She changed her moods quickly, just like a fairy.

"Do you understand what has happened, Gwen? You ate fairy food. Are you finding it hard to concentrate? To act normal? To be yourself?"

Gwen nodded reluctantly.

"You're half-in, half-out. That was the judgment by the time the row was settled. Your body dwells amongst mortals, but your spirit belongs to Faerie. You're being pushed and pulled between the two. You'll keep falling through the cracks. It can only get worse."

Gwen's blood ran cold, not only at what her cousin said, but at how she had said it. So calm and cool.

"You're not Findabhair," she accused. "You're a changeling, like in the stories, a fairy pretending to be human."

Findabhair shook her head. The sympathy in her eyes was the worst blow of all. Gwen so wanted to believe this wasn't her cousin.

"I know they're affecting me," Findabhair said quietly, "but I haven't changed that much. I was never one to mince my words. I'm telling you the truth, for your own sake. So you can save yourself. There's no danger to me. I've chosen to stay with them. If you would only do the same, everything would be fine!"

"This is crazy!" Gwen said, suddenly afraid.

She was shivering with cold and the beginning of shock. Things were topsy-turvy. Up until now, as far as Gwen was concerned, her sole mission had been to rescue Findabhair. Now suddenly the matter was turned on its head. Faerie was staking a claim to *her*! Once again, the King had out-maneuvered her. All Midir's warnings clamored in her mind even as the reversal sent her into a tailspin.

And adding to her upset was the secret wish inside, the quietly insidious urge to say *"Yes."*

"We can't just take off like this!" she argued frantically. "What about our parents, our friends, our lives? We were born to be human, not fairies. You've got to stop this and stop it now! It's crazy, you know it is!"

"Crazy?"

Findabhair's tone said it all. The familiar I-know-better-than-you confirmed she was no imposter.

"Look, Gwen, isn't this what you and I have been searching for ever since we were little? The Faraway Country? All our hopes and dreams? Here they are on a silver platter and you're turning them down! Who, I ask you, is the madwoman here?"

Gwen's head was spinning. It wasn't fair. No one should ever have to face this kind of choice. The Land of

Faerie shimmered with promise. And she knew there was more to the dream than met the eye—a hidden catch, like the hook in the worm—still, it tempted her.

Inside Gwen the battle raged, one voice crying out to join the fairies, the other quietly refusing to forsake her own world.

Findabhair sensed the conflict and spoke persuasively.

"I love my ordinary life too, but it's not as if I'll never see it again. I phoned Mum from town, by the way, and told her we're having a great time. Gwen, *everything* is possible when you're a magical being."

"That's not true," Gwen countered, "and you know it isn't. You can't have your cake and eat it too. You just end up with the crumbs. It's not possible to be in two places at the same time. You're only a visitor to our world now. You don't live here anymore."

"Midir fancies you, you know," Findabhair said, changing her tack. "We could be queens in Faerie together. Just imagine the *craic!*"

"I'm too young to get married!" Gwen yelled, furious with her cousin. It was bad enough trying to sort out the dilemma. The last thing she needed was a handsome young man being dangled as bait. "And so are you, Findabhair Folan! And neither you nor that tricksy boyfriend of yours is going to boss me around. You can't make me do what I don't want to do and that's that!"

Findabhair was taken aback by the force of Gwen's words.

"I'm not the only one who has changed, cuz."

The admiration in her voice calmed Gwen down. A thoughtful silence fell between the two. The memory of their long friendship rose like flames to warm them, reminding each of how much she liked the other. Both were reluctant to speak in case they broke the good mood.

"I brought your stuff," Findabhair said at last.

She pulled Gwen's knapsack from under a bush and handed it over, a peace offering.

"Thanks," Gwen muttered. "I'll never think of old ladies as harmless again."

Findabhair snickered. She went back to dabbling her feet in the stream. Gwen shuddered at the thought of the icy water. She joined her cousin on the bank but kept her shoes on.

"What is it with these guys anyway?" Gwen said lightly. "I mean, aside from the fact that we're beautiful and intelligent, what's the attraction?"

Her cousin laughed.

"Novelty, m'dear. They've been around for millennia. They know each other so well they'd die of boredom if it weren't for us. Humanity, I mean. Could you imagine a marriage lasting a thousand years? Then multiply that by a few thousand more!"

"I see your point." Gwen nodded. "So, are you still cooling the King's heels?"

Findabhair kicked her feet till the water foamed.

"Funny thing about that," she said softly. "You'll

think I'm full of myself when I say this, but I'm pretty sure he's falling in love with me." She smiled secretively at the frothing bubbles. "I don't think he intended to. It seems to be throwing him for a loop."

Gwen shook her head, bemused.

"Is this a dream or a nightmare or what?"

She had barely uttered the words when a blast of wind shook the trees around them. The fair folk had arrived. Dressed in tattered greens and browns, hair knotted with twigs, they were like a band of outlaws grinning at her. She looked for Midir, but he wasn't among them. The King stepped forward to catch hold of Findabhair, Robin Hood claiming his Maid Marian. Gwen saw the burning glance he gave her cousin.

Now he turned to Gwen with a courteous bow. His features were cool, his eyes aloof, but the voice was rich and dark like the night.

"Thou hast free will in this matter and thou hast not. Death is one of the penalties for those who come unbidden to us. Instead we grant thee life. Our life. To sleep in a mound is to place oneself under the sway of Faerie. Yet we were kind and did yield to thy choice not to join us. Thou didst pursue us and enter into our court. In sporting spirit we tempted thee. Thou wert warned not to eat of our food, yet thou didst eat. The judgment is fair. The decision is thine. Accept our rightful claim to thee or be banished to your own world, a wandering wraith.

"What dost thou say?"

Seventeen

Gwen was thinking fast. How was she going to get out of this one? Even she had to admit there was a strong case against her. Her cousin's eyes pleaded.

"I'm not saying yes and I'm not saying no," she began.

The King's features darkened. She finished hurriedly.

"I need to think about it. If you own eternity, what's a little time?"

True to his nature, Finvarra's temper transformed. A smile of approval lit up his features.

"You wish to continue the game?"

Gwen nodded. She held her breath as he considered the proposal.

"It has been good sport thus far."

With a royal wave of his hand, he made his decision.

"Granted. A little time. No more than a day of your own reckoning. We go to our northern kingdom by the Lake of Shadows. Join us there tomorrow's eve or accept your doom."

"Where?" Gwen asked him, glad of a reprieve however short. "I don't know Ireland very well."

Findabhair was about to answer, but the King cut her off.

"In your world it is called . . . ," he paused, mischievously, "island island."

The fairies burst into raucous laughter. Findabhair tried to speak again but in the blink of an eye she had vanished, along with the others.

Gwen stood alone in the forest night. *Island island.* Now what could that mean? Was it a trick? An anxious pang shot through her. Finvarra was a master trickster. She'd have to work hard to avoid his clutches.

But first, she needed sleep.

She looked around for a spot to camp down for the night. Piling up leaves to make a mattress, she spread out her ground sheet under an old apple tree. Snuggled inside her sleeping bag, she inhaled the scent of damp earth and greenery. The night noises of the forest played around her: the creak of branches, the sigh of leaves, the scurry of small creatures in the undergrowth. From time to time came the hoot of an owl or the call of a woodcock. The darkness seemed to gather round, pressing against her like black water. Her heart fluttered, small and nervous. Was she safe? All alone in the dark wood? Despite her fears, exhaustion won over and she closed her eyes.

In the deep of night she awoke. Emerging from the warm dark bath of sleep, she found herself drifting

upward. A thistledown on the breeze? Or was she a but-
terfly newly risen from her cocoon? She felt impossibly
tiny, like a speck of starlight. A sudden shift in the wind
sent her tumbling. Now she was caught in a moonbeam
as she continued to spin. The whirl of bright motes made
her dizzy with laughter.

Am I a fairy? she wondered.

Then, with a wondrous ache of joy, she felt the leaf-
thin pale-veined wings that fluttered from her shoulders.

"Gwenhyvar! Come dance with us!"

The voices echoed from everywhere. She was not only
surrounded by others of her kind—tiny, winged, and light
as air—but by every creature and spirit who lived in the
forest. Birds, insects, and animals had joined the throng.
Elemental beings quivered in the dimness. Sylphs dropped
from the air, dryads left their trees, and naiads rose up
from the stream, luminous and wet. Parting leaf from twig
and eyelid from slumber, anyone and everything was
awake in the night.

*To life we wake from the long-forgotten dream, the
beautiful mystery. The taste of existence is a drop of honey
on the tongue. So very young and so very old, we have gone
to seed and run wild with the wind.*

It was a dance of stars and flowers and souls. Gwen
stepped into the chain to become part of the whole. How
long she danced she couldn't know. Time branched like a
tree and each bud was eternity. She could feel the world
dissolve into myth.

Unto what is the journeying? What stitches the weave of the warp and the weft? What lies between the layers of every moment?

She felt happy and beyond hope. Hidden like a pearl in the shell of her being was a secret message. In the shadow of the forest, beneath the sky of stars, it was all so simple. This dance had begun in ancient days and would continue on forever and ever. All that belonged to life danced this dance together.

And though there was a moment, somewhere in the night, when she sensed the menace moving deep in the shadows, the dark thing that hunted her beyond the trees, she knew she was safe at the heart of the dance. She knew she was immortal.

Early the next morning, Gwen was awakened by a loud chorus of birds. Sunlight streamed onto her face through the branches of the apple tree. She felt refreshed and invigorated. Some wonderful dream had trailed away with the night, but its imprint of bliss still lingered in her mind. Jumping up, she stripped off her clothes to wash in the stream. The shock of cold made her whoop out loud, and she danced on the forest floor to dry herself off.

"I'm going fairy," she laughed, tucking leaves in her hair.

Despite the ultimatum hanging over her, Gwen had to admit she felt on top of the world. No matter how many obstacles he put in her path, the King had yet to defeat her. She knew in a way she had never known before that she was strong and courageous and capable of anything.

As she walked back through the forest to reach the road, she found herself smiling at everything around her. She felt as if she were greeting old friends. Those pale-yellow mushrooms with the tiny frills. Where had she seen them before? A picture flashed through her mind: herself under the shade of a golden umbrella, sharing a cup of nectar with a field mouse. Now she tripped over a gnarled stump. The twisted sculpture of root and wood looked like a statue of Pan. The moss was the green hair of a satyr's limb. Was that a wiry face bowed to the flute of a twig? Amused by her imaginings, Gwen hurried on. Behind her piped a trill of music.

Once on the road, she marched past the spot where the old woman had trapped her. With a jaunty toss of her head, she saluted the bush. And when she came to the ruined abbey of Boyle, she admired its airy grandness without a trace of dread.

Boyle itself was waking up for the day. Delivery vans pulled up at butchers, bakers, and grocery shops. With a rumble and clatter of metal, ale barrels were rolled into the cellars of pubs. Here and there, doors opened to usher out people on their way to work. Sleepy faces brightened at the touch of sunshine.

Gwen entered the pub cum tourist office in the hopes of finding Bernie. But there were no customers at that early hour. The proprietor stood alone, polishing glasses behind the bar.

"Excuse me," she asked him. "Is there a place in the north of Ireland called 'island island'?"

She could tell by his look that he was wondering about her. Then his face cleared.

"It's for the cryptic crossword in the *Irish Times*, is it?"

"Yes," she replied, though she had no idea what he was talking about.

He scratched his beard with concentration, then went into the kitchen to question his wife. He returned in triumph.

"Inch Island," he declared. "In the northern county of Donegal. 'Inch' is an English derivation of *Inis*, which is 'island' in Irish. Inch Island. Island island. How's that for you? The wife has brains to burn."

"Great. Thanks," said Gwen. After a moment's hesitation, she threw all pretense to the wind. "So, how do I get there?"

Eighteen

Gwen's high spirits stayed with her on the journey north despite the "in-between" state Findabhair had warned her about. Luckily, most of the day was spent in transit. Slipping between the worlds wasn't too great a problem while sitting on a bus, though buying her ticket had been another story. She was certain the young man who sold it to her had no idea of the stone window that arched behind him. Through it she had glimpsed a lady's chamber draped with tapestries. There was a high bed with a white lace canopy and a fire burning in the grate. A golden harp rested in a corner against the wall. Gwen could only wonder to whom it belonged.

But even the bus ride was unsettling at times. Into the endless parade of green hills, stone walls, new bungalows, and old cottages strange sights kept intruding. The silhouette of white towers gleamed in the distance. Cloaked figures walked over a rainbow as if it were a bridge. On a faraway hill, light fell like spears on a lone tree hung with gold and silver apples. Sometimes she heard music, a piper piping away, and the music was so sad it brought tears to her eyes.

Gwen began to worry that she was on a never-ending journey. Was she trapped on the bus, traveling forever? She was sure they had crossed that wide river before. And the ruined castle with the broken gate looked familiar too. But there was no way she could tell for certain. She was a stranger in a strange land. No landmarks or signposts could place her on the map. The road itself seemed to shift and change. Most of the time it was a modern highway, a smooth line of gray tarmac crossing the countryside. But sometimes it was a tortuous track, rough and potholed, hemmed in by trees that scraped the window. Then the sleek and air-conditioned vehicle would turn into its ancestor, something rickety, juddering, and claustrophobic.

Gwen had just decided to get off the bus as soon as possible, when something happened to change her mind.

She sensed the vision before it came. A profound silence fell over the bus, like a heavy blanket. The hum of the engine suddenly ceased, along with the chatter of the other passengers. Everything seemed to be eerily suspended. Then she saw it, outside her window, moving swiftly and silently through the traffic. An ebony coach drawn by great black horses. The horses' eyes were pale and blind. There was no driver. As the carriage drew up alongside Gwen, she could see its occupants. Two figures sat in the dim interior. One was Finvarra in midnight colors, the kingly star aglow on his brow. The other was her cousin, slender and still, draped in dark veils. Findabhair's face was as pale as moonlight, her eyes distant. Gwen tapped on the window and tried to call out. Her cousin didn't respond, didn't even look at her. Then the black coach moved on, speeding into the north.

Gwen knew she had no choice but to follow. That brief cold glimpse had showed her deepest dread. Findabhair was leaving this world behind. She was shedding her mortal self.

It was late afternoon when Gwen arrived in the village of Burnfoot. A cluster of buildings straggled along the one main street: a small inn, post office, chip shop, and grocery. All around rolled the hills of Donegal, purpled with heather. The air was damp with the hint of rain and the sea beyond.

She went into the shop to ask for directions.

"No, you won't be needing a boat to Inch," she was told. "There's a causeway to the island as good as a road. You might have to walk it, unless a car passes you by. First left outside the village, go along a twisty road, then left again and you're on the Embankment."

"Is there a place to stay on the island?"

"Oh aye. The Clan House of the O'Dohertys takes in visitors. It's run by one of your own and open all year round."

As she left the village, Gwen was met by a little boy on a tricycle. The impish face grinned up at her from beneath a mop of black curls. His eyes were bright with mischief. He held out his hand to offer an apple, dark red and shining.

"Oh thank you!" she said, enchanted. "Aren't you cute?"

The fruit was the first thing she had felt like eating in ages. But she had no sooner bit into the crisp skin than the child crowed with delight.

"Tonight you will play with me on *Magh Abhlach*. The Plain of the Apple Trees!"

Gwen dropped the apple as if it hid a worm.

"What did you say?"

The boy was already speeding away, legs pedaling with all the urgency of childhood. She stared after him, bewildered. Was he a little kid talking about an orchard? Or was he a fairy child sent to trick her? The collision of worlds was taking its toll. How could she know for certain? Everyone and everything came under suspicion.

Or was she just being paranoid?

But something *had* happened.

And Gwen grew aware of it as she trudged down the road. The dense hedges of hawthorn seemed to close in on her. The cloying scent of greenery made her cough. A cloud of midges swarmed at her head. When she tried to outrun them her legs dragged heavily, as if she were wading through water. Her knapsack felt like a bag of bricks. It became a struggle to put one foot in front of the other; but at last she reached the causeway.

The moment Gwen stepped onto the Embankment,

she recovered instantly. A wholesome breeze blew across the water. Ducks and swans moved over the smooth surface. Behind her ranged the ridge of mountains that formed a barrier between Lough Swilly and Lough Foyle. Her gaze settled on the cashel that crowned a high hill, the ancient stone fort called the Grianán of Aileach. Once she would have been eager to explore it; now she shivered at the sight of its jagged silhouette. Would she make her last stand behind those walls?

She had no doubt about the nature of the struggle ahead. Though much was shrouded in mystery, Midir's warnings and her own premonitions pointed to one thing: her life and her cousin's hung in the balance.

And despite the distractions of the journey north, she had come up with some tactics to deal with the fairies. The least likely to work was a desperate speech about freedom, an attempt to appeal to their good side. More probable was the proposal of a time-sharing compromise, the kind she had read about in various tales. She and Findabhair could spend some of the year in Faerie—their holidays perhaps—and the rest in their own world.

The bottom line? She was planning to fight. Her true hope and intention was a daring escape, dragging her cousin along whether Findabhair liked it or not. Gwen was depending on Midir to help her out, or at least to create a diversion. And there was something else she was counting on. Her secret weapon. A weakness she had detected in her adversary. It was Findabhair who had mentioned it, the last time they had met, and Gwen had seen it herself in the King's fiery glance. *I'm pretty sure he's falling in love with me. I don't think he intended to. It seems to be throwing him for a loop.* The King had used Gwen's love of food against her; she hoped to do the same with his love for her cousin. A soft spot always left room to maneuver and manipulate.

I can do this, she assured herself, as she marched smartly across the causeway.

But no sooner had she reached the other side than the dreadful lethargy returned. Were the fairies jinxing her? She looked back over the causeway she had just crossed. Lake water lapped against the sides of the Embankment. Of course! Didn't Findabhair say the fairies had less power near water?

But she couldn't stay there. She had to move on.

Gwen didn't get far on the island road. After the brief respite of well-being, the sluggishness felt even worse. Her feet were like blocks of concrete. Despite all her efforts to keep going, her legs finally buckled. Unable to stop herself, she fell on the road.

As she lay there struggling in vain to get up, a cyclist came speeding around the corner. He tried to stop the moment he saw her. Too late, he skidded and lost control of his bike, toppling over with a crash.

"Jesus, Mary, and Joseph. What the—"

Swearing vociferously, he extricated himself from the tangle of wheels and handlebars. Then he saw that Gwen was still slumped on the road.

"Good God, did I hit you?"

Gwen stared helplessly up at the distraught young man. His nut-brown hair framed strong and handsome features. There was a friendly look to the startling green eyes. His voice rang with panic.

"Are you hurt? Are you in pain?"

She tried to speak but no sound came out. He managed to get her onto her feet, but her legs were rubbery and she collapsed again. Frantically he searched for some hidden wound.

The situation was so absurd Gwen might have laughed if she could. She was like a rag doll. Though her mind was clear, she had no control whatsoever over her body. And here was this good-looking boy, not much older than herself, going crazy with worry.

"I'll take you to Granny's," he decided. "She'll know what to do."

He removed Gwen's knapsack and left it with his bicycle in the shelter of the hedgerow. Then hoisting her over his shoulders in a fireman's carry, he set off down the road.

Gwen's line of vision trailed upside down. The winding road was lined with hedges of fuchsia. Their blossoms looked like fat red-and-purple bees. Through the gaps in the hedge she could see grassy fields roll down to the coast. Feeling like a sack of potatoes, she worried about her weight on the young man's back. But his broad shoulders seemed to bear her easily.

When they reached a whitewashed cottage with a

neatly thatched roof, he set her down. A crooked path wound through an unruly garden of flowers and vegetables. Herbs grew in window boxes lining the sills. Turf lay stacked against the side wall. Yellow celandine trailed over the door that was already open.

There stood an old lady, tall and regal, with gray hair tied back from her face. She was dressed in faded dungarees. Her short-sleeved blouse showed strong arms brown and mottled from the sun. She wore no jewelery except for a silver Claddagh ring on her left hand. Her eyes were the same sea-green as the boy's, though a lighter shade. They narrowed as she took in Gwen's plight.

"What have you brought us, Dara?" Granny asked quietly.

She helped him bring Gwen into the house. They laid her on a daybed in the kitchen. Dara described the accident, insisting that he hadn't hit her. Granny checked her over and declared nothing broken, then gazed for a time into the girl's eyes.

"It's some kind of shock," Dara said, running his hand through his hair. "She's a tourist, I think. She has a haversack and sleeping roll. I left them by the road with my pushbike. I'll go and get them. Maybe a passport or something will tell us who she is."

Gwen was beginning to feel the first inkling of terror. No matter how hard she tried, she couldn't communicate with them.

Granny saw the fear and placed a cool hand on the girl's brow.

"You'll be fine, ashy-pet. You're safe with us."

Dara frowned at Granny.

"Shouldn't we get a doctor? If she's a foreigner, it might be best if you didn't treat her. This could be a bad business altogether."

Granny shook her head.

"No odds where she comes from, medicine won't help her. Not the new kind, anyway. There's a *pisreog* on her, of that I am certain. It wasn't you that struck her but a fairy dart."

Though Dara looked surprised, he didn't argue. He obviously respected the old woman's opinion.

With her mind made up, Granny spoke brusquely.

"Go collect her things and your bike. On the way back, bring me branches from the ash tree and the whitethorn that grows on the Fargan Knowe. Take care as you pass the lone bush on the hill near the hollow. It's a *skeog*. If the fairies are there, they may try to stop you."

"I am the island king. They will not hinder me."

"Perhaps not. But your kingship will surely be tested tonight. By the looks of things, they will come for her soon."

Gwen was beginning to wonder if she were hallucinating. Was she putting words into their mouths to suit her predicament? The old lady looked like a retired schoolteacher or librarian. Was she really calling the boy a king? Surely that wasn't possible in present-day Ireland even if one ignored the blue jeans and Thin Lizzy T-shirt. Had the fairies finally pushed her over the edge?

When Dara left, Granny bent over Gwen. Her expression was both stern and kind.

"I could bring in a modern doctor, my dear, but it would do you no good. My name is Grania Harte. I am a fairy doctress. I don't expect you to understand that term, for few know of the magical arts in this day and age. But you couldn't have got into this hubble without some misadventure with the fey folk. There is no one who can help you if I do not."

Well what do you know, Gwen thought to herself. She's a witch.

Nineteen

Granny Harte's kitchen was like herself, a bemusing mix of the odd and the ordinary. One wall was dominated by a hearth which held a black cauldron. The other accommodated a refrigerator and an electric stove. The floor was a chessboard of red and black flagstones. From the wooden beams of the ceiling hung dried bunches of herbs, and strings of onions and garlic. A portable television was squeezed onto a shelf crammed with crockery jars labeled by hand: *adderstongue, nightshade, hemlock, martagon, agrimony, eyebright, eglantine.* Was that an astrolabe beside the toaster? A large speckled toad peeped out from the enameled sink. In the corner near the door leaned an ancient besom broom. Above it hung a calendar from the Bank of Ireland.

Granny moved about the kitchen with quiet purpose. There was something wolflike about her—the gray hair, the wiry form, the pointed features. Though she appeared to be engaged in domestic tasks, her actions hinted of a secret power. She lit a fire in the grate with newspaper and matches. As she tossed various herbs into the flames, the room filled with a sweet-smelling smoke. At the stove she stirred a big pot, brewing up a potion that smelled sour and heavy.

Unable to move, Gwen could do no more than watch, but she felt reassured. Granny's air of authority inspired confidence. When a cup was placed to Gwen's lips, she did her best to swallow. The murky liquid was not unpleasant, as peppermint and honey cloaked something tart.

"At the heart of this potion," the old woman explained, "is the root of the elder boiled with the root of an apple tree that bears red fruit. It will expel any inimical spirit. You'll go into a fever but do not be alarmed. It is to break the hold of fairy influence."

The drink coursed through Gwen like liquid fire. Immediately her body began to twitch, first with itchy prickles, then aches and pains. As the jabs grew sharper, she uttered little cries. She knew she was being cured and tried hard to endure it, but she couldn't stop the tears from trickling down her face. She longed to be at home in her own bed, being nursed by her mother. Not suffering helplessly in this house of strangers.

When Dara came in, he stood beside her and looked down with pity.

"Poor wean," he said. "I would take it for you if I could."

The sea-green eyes were warm and kind. She stared

mutely back at him, feeling a little better. Strangers, yes, but good ones.

"Have you the branches?" Granny asked him.

"Lashin's of them. On my pushbike."

"Wreathe the door and the windows. Then strew this bag of primroses over sill and threshold. They were gathered on May Eve, so they are very potent. These will keep out the Wee Folk. My only fear is that they will call up something older and more perilous."

Dara stood straighter. His voice was steady.

"Rare are the times my kingship comes into use. I am ready to defend her."

"Have you your scepter?"

He nodded. "I will keep it near."

It was dark by the time they were finished their work. Night pressed against the windows like black water. An urgency crept into Granny's ministrations. At the four corners of Gwen's bed, she placed a lighted candle, a glass beaker of water, a bowl of salt, and a vessel of earth. Now she stood at the fire that had fallen to red ash. One by one, she tossed three stones into the embers, calling out as she threw.

"The first stone I cast is for the head in mad fever. The second stone I cast is for the heart in mad fever. The third stone I cast is for the back in mad fever. Let the mind, soul, and will be free."

Gwen was burning up. She could feel herself slipping into delirium. Dara and Granny sat in chairs beside her.

Their features were strained. The air was fraught with tension. What terrible thing might come to claim her?

"Be of good courage," Granny said quietly. "You do not face this alone. The king and I are with you."

The suspense was torment in itself. When the first sounds came, it was almost a relief. For better or worse, this was it.

There was a scampering of feet, like a dog outside. The door handle rattled. Muffled cries of dismay. Whatever was out there scuttled sideways, from the door to the window. A tap on the pane. More angry whispers.

Dara and Granny sat without moving. Gwen shivered uncontrollably.

Now an unseen prowler circled the cottage. The noise it made was horrible. There was a creaking as of some jointed thing, and it appeared to be dragging a large object in tow. From time to time it let out a howl that curdled the blood. Yet despite the clamor, nothing entered the house. The way was barred. After what seemed an interminable length of time, the sounds faded away.

Dara let out a sigh and went to stand up, but Granny shook her head. It wasn't over. Gwen's shallow breaths rasped the air.

A great thud suddenly struck the door, as if a body had been hurled against it. The three of them jumped. The blow was followed by prolonged battering, like that of a gigantic fist.

A voice cried out, chilling and dreadful.

"OPEN! OPEN!"

"Who goes there?" Granny called back. "No guests are welcome tonight!"

The door burst open. A cold gust of wind rushed into the room. Dishes rattled in the cupboard. The curtains flapped wildly. The fire in the grate roared into life.

A giantess stepped into the kitchen. Black-mantled, tall and threatening, she had eyes that burned like red-and-black coals. The most awful thing about her was the single horn that protruded from her forehead. It was thick and curved like a scimitar. The baleful eyes surveyed the room.

"Who are you?" Granny demanded.

"I am the Witch of the One Horn."

The monstrous apparition turned away to crouch by the hearth. From her cloak she produced a ball of pale yarn and began to toss it in her hands with violent motions. Then she paused to cry out.

"WHERE ARE MY SISTERS?"

Immediately another giantess entered the room. She also had a loathsome and terrifying aspect. Dressed the same as the first, she had two horns on her head and whiskers that jutted from her chin like a beard.

"Give me place!" she screeched. "I am the Witch of the Two Horns."

The second witch had no sooner joined the first than a third came in. Her skin was blotched with livid marks.

She bore three horns like a hideous crown. She, too, hunkered beside her sisters.

Writhing and convulsing to some unseen tune, the three began to enact a sinister ritual.

The first witch unwound the ball of yarn and, twisting it around her horn, passed it on to the second. She, in turn, strung the skein across her two horns, then gave it to the third. That sister did likewise before returning it to the first. Again and again they spun the thread on their horns, increasing their movements to a horrible speed. Illumined by the red glow of the hearth, their shadows danced on the walls, grotesque and eldritch.

Gwen was suffering the worst nightmare of her life. As the witches pulled and twisted the skein, she felt her insides contort in turn. Her life force was being stretched, as if on the rack, and impaled on the horns of the terrible sisters. She opened her mouth to scream, but no sound came out.

The witches intoned, one after the other, a ghastly dialogue of ill intent.

"She was born into this world."

"She is called to another."

"Split the thread between the two."

"It is too thin."

"It will break."

"Then cut it short."

"And let her be forfeit."

"To the one who claims her."

At that very moment, Granny signaled to Dara and

they rushed to the fire. Before the witches could move, both had joined the circle and caught onto the thread.

On the daybed, Gwen felt a brief respite, a slackening of the tension that was wrenching her apart.

In a calm high voice, Granny called out:

"I, Grania Harte, Wise Woman of Inch, claim this thread for my house and hearth."

Dara spoke next, clear and forceful.

"I, Dara McCrory, King of Inch, claim this thread for my land and territories."

Now the battle was joined, a war of will, the old woman and young man versus the three witches. Caught in between, Gwen's life was the thread that was held in the balance.

The contest was harrowing. Even as they struggled, Gwen's torment worsened, but it seemed the pain was now being shared. Granny's features turned a sickly gray. Dara's eyes were wild and a muscle worked in his jaw, clenched with effort. Then came the moment when Gwen realized the truth. They were losing the battle. She could sense her defenders weakening under the strain. They couldn't hold on. The thread was being slowly torn from their fingers.

She felt the anguish of their defeat, their despair. Then, to her surprise, she sensed something else. Their ferocious resolve to fight on. They wouldn't back down, not even if it killed them. They were willing to sacrifice their lives for hers.

Inspired by their heroics, Gwen found her own courage. Even as she urged them to let go, to save themselves, another truth struck her. Dara and Granny were losing because they were outnumbered. Two battled three. But a third might level the playing field. If she could join the struggle, they had a chance.

Now Gwen delved deep inside herself for that last ounce of strength only the brave can muster. This was not just for her, but for her champions as well. *I can do it,* she swore. For a moment, it seemed, she no longer lay in bed but stood at the heart of a raging battlefield. Her will-to-power roused, she lifted her sword.

No sooner had the other two sensed her presence in the fight than they rallied anew. Three wills now fought against the three witches. The tide had turned. Slowly but surely the dreadful sisters backed down. Now Granny and Dara freed the thread from their horns. Now the witches let out an abominable shriek. A chorus of howls echoed outside. Still shrieking and keening, the three fled from the house till their wails dwindled on the wind, far in the distance.

Dara and Granny stood by the fire, the skein of life still entwined in their hands. With infinite care they bore it over to Gwen, who was in the final throes of her fever. As they gently laid the thread upon her, it dispelled like mist and her fever broke. Flooded with peace, she drifted into a merciful sleep.

Later that night, Gwen's eyes fluttered open to see

dark figures in front of the fire. After a pang of fright, she realized that they were Dara and Granny. The two sat together with cups of tea, talking in low voices.

"What will we say to her? She can't possibly understand these matters."

"She knows something, Dara. She has gone among them, of that I am certain. But the true question remains: why were the Horned Ones called to claim her? No matter what, we must speak truthfully to her, for she deserves our respect. Few are those who could have survived this night. We will not pretend it didn't occur."

Gwen tried to wake. She wanted to join them, to talk about what had happened. She knew she was finally free of the fairies and in a safe house. Too weak and worn-out from her ordeal, she fell back asleep even as a last thought niggled in her mind.

What about Findabhair?

Twenty

The smell of sausages frying in the pan woke Gwen up, along with the rumblings of an appetite she hadn't felt for ages. The kitchen seemed to dazzle, with fresh air and sunshine streaming through the windows. Granny Harte stood at the stove, a flowered apron around her waist.

The scene was so cozy and normal that Gwen wondered a moment if the night's horrors hadn't been a dream, a fevered nightmare caused by illness. She shook her head. She knew too much about that other reality to dismiss it so easily.

When Granny turned to check on her, Gwen spoke directly.

"Thank you for saving my life."

The old woman blinked at her frankness, then smiled broadly.

"You're very welcome, my dear. I was just doing my job. If you'd like to wash before breakfast, the bathroom is down the hall to your left. Your clothes are in the airing cupboard. I took them out of your haver-sack."

In the washroom, Gwen was surprised by the bright yellow fittings and fluffy towels. She giggled to herself. What had she expected from a fairy doctress? Slugs and snails and puppy dogs' tails? After her shower, she dressed in clean jeans and a pink T-shirt. Combing her hair, she hummed beneath her breath. She felt wonderfully well.

"What doesn't kill you makes you stronger," she told her mirrored image.

When she returned to the kitchen, Granny set a big plate in front of her heaped with rashers, sausages, egg, and fried mushrooms. There was also homemade soda bread and a pot of strong tea. Gwen tucked into the feast with gusto.

"My name is Gwen Woods," she said, between mouthfuls. "I think I owe you an explanation."

"Eat first, then we can chat. Dara is gathering sea-weed for my garden and will join us soon."

When Dara came in, Gwen went suddenly shy. The young man leaned against the door frame as he removed his wellingtons. Then he rolled up his shirtsleeves to wash his hands at the sink. He was very good-looking. She hadn't imagined *that*. His brown hair fell loosely around finely honed features. The sea-green eyes had an open friendly gaze.

"You're looking well," he said with a slightly crooked grin, as he sat down at the table.

Granny handed him his breakfast. Gwen was glad she had finished hers. She would have been too self-conscious to eat in front of him.

"Now, pet," said Granny, as she sat down at the table and poured fresh tea, "are you ready to tell us how you came to be fairy-struck on Inch Island?"

After everything they had done for her, Gwen felt compelled to tell her story from beginning to end. Despite her embarrassment at parts, she left nothing out: the bus accident and the leprechaun; the abduction of Findabhair from Tara; her own lonely travels around Ireland; the tests and trials she had endured; the many traps and close escapes; the moment of her great failure when she ate fairy food . . .

Even as she told her tale, Gwen's discomfiture grew. She had been so careless and stupid, broken so many rules, made so many mistakes. In the end she had brought her problems into their house and endangered their lives. What could they think of her?

Granny nodded thoughtfully.

"Just as I suspected. There was a fairy dart in the apple the little boy gave you. Finvarra was taking no chances you'd be strong enough to fight him. You were holding your own quite nicely till then."

Her tone of approval was unmistakable. The same admiration shone in Dara's eyes, with an added hint of envy.

"What adventures you've been having! And well met, despite the hardship. You're a great girl altogether."

As she blushed at his praise, a stray thought crossed her mind. She was glad Findabhair wasn't there.

"Has your cousin chosen to stay in Faerie?"

Something behind Granny's question put Gwen on guard.

"She loves it there, but that isn't the point. She can't stay. She's human, not fairy. I intend to drag her out whether she likes it or not."

Dara and Granny exchanged glances.

"It's not as simple as that," Dara said. "There are rules and customs that govern what goes on between us and the Good Folk. You can't come and go as you please with them."

"You mean she's a prisoner? They won't let her out?!"

Granny sighed. "As Dara says, it's not that simple. There are protocols concerning visits to Faerie, regardless of whether you go by choice or not. The most common period is seven years. For those who are stolen, the minimum is a year and a day, the traditional length of time for lifting a curse or a spell. Many of our kind have entered Faerie of their own free will, but even more have been abducted—young men to take part in their sports, new mothers to wet-nurse their babies, beautiful girls to be the King's bride . . ."

The old woman's sight clouded a moment, then she continued.

"The fairies bless whomever goes among them with

special gifts. Many a famous Irish musician has 'gone abroad' to return with the plaintive airs of Faerie. Other visitors are given wonder tales to delight this world, or the lore of healing with herbs and plants. If a visit goes badly, if a human tries to trick the fairies or steal their riches, he or she can suffer ill health and bad luck, even sickness unto death."

The more she heard, the more anxious Gwen grew.

"Are you saying Findabhair will be there for *at least* a year and a day?"

"It's not such a terrible thing," Granny said quietly. "I myself lived in Faerie for a spell of time. That is how I acquired my knowledge and arts and my title of 'Wise Woman.'"

Gwen mulled over her words, but she couldn't shake the feeling that there was more, something the old lady was keeping from her.

"My cousin is changing," she said slowly. "Each time I see her, she seems more like them. Less human."

Now she remembered what nagged at the back of her mind, an image that embodied her greatest concern. The black coach with Findabhair silent inside, cloaked in veils, pale as moonlight.

As she described the vision to Granny and Dara, she studied their faces. What she saw there confirmed her suspicion. They couldn't hide the truth. She had read too many tales.

"It was the Death Coach, wasn't it?"

Gwen's tone was level, more a statement than a question.

Dara looked sad and couldn't meet her eyes.

"Some choose to stay in Faerie forever," the Wise Woman said softly. She paused before she finished. "To live in one world, one must die in the other."

Gwen's face went white. She felt the shock threatening to undermine her resolve, but she pushed it aside.

"I'm not going to let her die! I'm sticking to my original plan. I'm going in for her."

"And we'll go with you!" Dara pledged. He grinned at Granny. "Won't we?"

When the old woman didn't respond immediately, Gwen spoke up.

"There's no need to. Honestly, I can do this myself. You've done so much—"

Granny raised her hand before Gwen could say more.

"Fools rush in where angels fear to tread. I do not take these decisions lightly. But I would not let you go without my aid." She frowned at Dara. "We will have to outwit the masters of trickery."

He nodded. "You haven't said anything about the Hunter's—?"

"No need to speak of it," Granny broke in, "unless it's necessary. We have our hands full as it is. We won't add to our worries if it isn't the time. I will cast a fairy calendar today. Why don't the two of you take a picnic and go for a dander around the island? I need to be alone.

Show Gwen the shelly beach, Dara, and the old fort and the Cairn. Keep clear of the fairy fort at Dunfinn. If Finvarra is on Inch, that's where he'll be.

"Enjoy yourselves, now, before we face what we must. Something tells me our troubles have only begun."

Twenty-one

T he narrow road hugged the coastline of Inch, rising and falling with the hilly landscape. Fields of heather and wild broom rolled down to rocky shores and inlets curved with sandy beaches. The island lay in the crook of Lough Swilly, a slender arm of the northern sea. Shadowing the horizon were the mainland mountains of Inishowen, gray-blue with cloud and mist.

"That's Gollan Hill," Dara told her, "and the dark one behind is the Scalp. The islanders have a saying. 'When the Scalp puts on her nightcap, Inch may look out.'"

"Meaning?" asked Gwen.

"Storm clouds on the summit and we're in for bad weather."

They strolled together along the sunny road, carrying a picnic basket and a rolled-up blanket. Dara pointed out the various sights as they went.

"That green track leads to Dunfinn, the island's fairy fort. Do you see how it trails to the left of the whin and the hawthorn? The 'sinister' or left-handed way is the path to Faerie. This height ahead of us with the stand of trees is the Fargan Knowe. The windiest spot on the island. There's a name on every part of Inch, it's so well known and loved."

His manner was easygoing, without shyness or reserve. At one point he picked a wild daisy to tuck behind her ear. He was so charming and handsome, she tripped over her words. But if he noticed the effect he had on her, he didn't show it. He obviously enjoyed entertaining her and looked pleased whenever he made her laugh.

They reached a level place with a commanding view. Gwen admired the cream-colored mansion that graced the site.

"Does that belong to the local gentry?"

Dara sputtered with laughter.

"Actually, it's the milkman's house."

"Score one for modern Ireland," she said, laughing too.

"You have a brilliant laugh."

Now the road plunged downward, hurrying them along to a small pier where fishing boats were moored. The trawlers gently nosed the dock, like dolphins. A tangle of nets lay drying in the sun.

They rambled over to the strand nearby and removed their shoes and socks. The shore was strewn with shells, driftwood, and knotted seaweed. Bird prints inscribed the sand like tiny hieroglyphics. The water lapped gently over their bare feet.

"Why didn't I bring my bathing suit?" Gwen groaned.

"Afraid to get wet?"

He was too quick, she had no time to defend herself. Before she could stop him, he had hauled her into the sea and dunked her. She gasped at the bite of the ice-cold water. Some of it went up her nose and into her mouth. She righted herself, coughing and choking.

"Are you all right?" he asked, suddenly contrite.

All shyness fled; her honor was at stake. This was no time to be a shrinking violet. As he leaned over her anxiously, she grabbed him in a headlock and pushed him under the waves. She was still screeching with laughter by the time he recovered.

They wrestled and splashed till they were soaked to the skin. Dripping like seaweed, they waded out of the water and flung themselves down on the sand.

Gwen lay with her eyes closed, basking in the sun. Her clothes clung stickily as they dried in the heat. She grinned to herself. She had never felt so good. When Dara moved away, she sat up.

He was walking along the shore, as if looking for something. Then he picked up a stone and began to draw in the sand.

She was about to join him when something caught her eye. A dark shape on the horizon, rising up from the lough. She squinted against the glare in an effort to see, but whatever it was vanished. A bird, or maybe a seal? She felt a prickle of unease. She would have told Dara, but as soon as she caught up with him it went out of her head.

He had written their names in the sand.

"Will I put a heart around them?"

His tone was friendly, his eyes bright with mischief. She couldn't tell if he was serious or teasing. She shrugged, and gave him a long look. His clothes were drenched, but he didn't seem to mind. A crown of sea wrack lay askew on his head. The slippery strands glistened darkly, like his dark-brown hair and sea-green eyes.

"Are you really a king?"

He returned her gaze without blinking.

"I am king of this island."

He began to trace a heart around their names, talking as he worked.

"There are many such kings in Ireland, on Tory, Aran, and other islands. It means nothing officially, though in some places we have special rights or duties—distributing the post from the mail boat, or opening regattas and patterns."

"Only kings? No queens?"

"Not that I know of. But the kings come through the female line. My uncle, my mother's brother, was king before me. He died in a motor accident. My sister's son will be king after me. As I said, it doesn't mean anything nowadays, but the older generation acknowledge me in their own way. They give me gifts at Christmas and

Easter, and sometimes I'm asked to mediate in quarrels between neighbors."

He finished the heart and stood with his hands on his hips, grinning at her.

"It means much more to the fairy folk. The hereditary kings are the only human rulers they recognize. They have no time for the *Taoiseach* at all." He started to laugh and at Gwen's puzzled look, explained. "The *Taoiseach* is our elected Prime Minister. The Good People only follow the old bloodlines."

Gwen was no longer surprised that someone could speak of fairies and prime ministers in one breath. Nor did she find it hard to consider Dara a king. Despite his casual manner, there was something special about him. He had a quality that inspired respect and loyalty. But what was she to make of this heart in the sand?

"I know a good place for a picnic," he said.

Collecting their basket and blanket, they headed back to the pier. Dara helped her over the low stone wall nearby.

"Isn't this private property?" she asked.

"Yes and no. It's the old fort. Military, not fairy. First built in Napoleon's time and then restored in World War One. A New Age community lives in it now. *Meitheal* they call themselves, the Irish word for 'working together.' They don't mind visitors."

On the other side of the wall was a grassy demesne with renovated brick buildings, groves of rowan and oak, a walled garden with an apple orchard, and winding paths fashioned of seashells and stones. The buildings were painted with Celtic designs, spirals like eyes and snakes swallowing their tails. Little children played naked in front of the houses. Clothes flapped on the washing lines. A polytunnel of translucent plastic sheltered fruits and vegetables.

"They come from all over the world," Dara explained. "Australia, Italy, Germany, North America, and Ireland too. The islanders think of them as hippies, but they aren't really. They believe in all kinds of things, including fairies, but they use computers and other modern technology."

Gwen shook her head.

"I had no idea so many people believed in fairies. But really, Dara, are you telling me most people do?"

Dara laughed.

"Irish people you mean? They do and they don't. Let's face it, what has Faerie to do with jobs and politics, new roads or farming? The two worlds have never been so far apart. But you wouldn't find many country people willing to cut down trees on a fairy fort. Not for love nor money."

They had reached the outer perimeter of the fort where grass-grown turrets and tunnels brooded over Lough Swilly. The cliffs sheered to cold waters below. Waves crashed against the mossy rocks. The shrill screech of seagulls pierced the air. Across the water, a sweep of mountains sheltered the town of Rathmullan. The wind carried the salty tang of the Atlantic beyond.

Choosing a spot on the grassy height, they spread out

the blanket and unpacked their picnic. They had cheese-and-tomato sandwiches on homemade bread, slices of cold ham and turkey, a jar of vinaigrette artichokes, two crunchy red apples, and a punnet of strawberries. For drinks they had a flask of hot chocolate and two bottles of lemonade. As they enjoyed the feast, talking and laughing, neither noticed the shadow that moved on the surface of the lough.

Gwen munched thoughtfully on an apple.

"It's weird for me to think of others believing in fairies, except for my cousin of course. I mean, Faerie was always my own little fantasy. I dreamed of it because I wasn't that happy with reality. Too ordinary, too boring, too . . . lonely."

Dara was stretched out on the blanket, resting his head on his hand.

"I like the way you think. Most girls are only interested in clothes and makeup."

Gwen was quick to retort.

"That's not true. Girls just don't tell boys what they think about, because most boys don't want to know. They back away if you're too smart. So we pretend we're not."

Dara sat up.

"Have you done that?"

She paused a moment before answering.

"No. But I think that's one of the reasons I've never had a boyfriend."

She pulled at the grass.

Dara looked surprised.

"I can't believe no one has fancied you!"

Gwen colored at the compliment, and remembered Midir. How quickly her life had changed that summer!

"Well, one person has," she admitted.

"I knew it." Dara grinned. "You're very pretty."

He regarded her thoughtfully and reached out to touch her hair where it shone in the sunlight.

"*Tá do ghruaig chomh fionn le ór agus do shúile gorm chomh le loch.*"

"What?"

"Your hair is fair like gold," he said softly, "and your eyes are as blue as the lough."

She drew back, uncomfortable.

"What's wrong?" he asked.

"Don't you think . . ." She bit her lip. "I'm over-weight?"

He looked surprised again.

"You're not skin and bones, if that's what you mean. You're lovely. I couldn't help but notice when your clothes were wet."

Gwen blushed furiously but was delighted all the same.

He leaned toward her.

"I've never met anyone like you," he said. "Intelligent, courageous . . ."

She smiled with sudden mischief.

"Maybe I like you because you're good-looking."

She amazed herself. Was she becoming a flirt? But

here was truly the reason she liked him. He was so easy to talk to, she could tease him as well.

He let out a loud laugh. "I hope you also respect my mind."

They laughed together, then it happened naturally. Both drew near to kiss.

"Better make that two," said Dara.

"Two kisses?"

"Two people who fancy you. And, yes, the other as well."

Twenty-two

As they left the fort and wandered back to the road, Dara took Gwen's hand. Thrilled, she grinned to herself as she imagined how she looked walking casually with a "boyfriend."

"I could run up a mountain without stopping for breath," she said.

He squeezed her hand to show he knew what she meant and that he felt the same way.

"We could climb the Cairn. There's a path nearby."

Inch Top, known locally as "the Cairn," was the highest point on the island. Sheep grazed in the lower pastures, but the way grew stonier and steeper the higher they went. Below them spread fields dotted with white cottages. Beyond, in the distance, seabirds circled rocky coves. Where the sun struck the cold waters of Lough Swilly, a mist of light and shadow whispered over the surface.

"Some people call it the Lake of Shadows," Dara told her, "but it's really the Lake of Eyes. Swilly is the English pronunciation for Súiligh. *Súil* is Irish for 'eye.' There's a legend about a sea serpent who dwells at the bottom of the lough, called Súileach—'full of eyes.'"

"Like the Loch Ness monster!" said Gwen. With a shiver of foreboding, she scanned the lake. It was smooth and glassy; there was nothing there. Her attention turned back to Dara. "You know so much about this place. You really love it, don't you?"

"It can be pretty lonesome in the winter. Wild winds and storms. Sometimes the Embankment's washed out and we're an island again. But rain or shine, I spend as much time as I can here."

"What? I thought you lived here!"

"Not at'all. My parents moved to Galway before I was born. I stay with Granny when I'm here and do odd jobs for her, and we all come up for Christmas. She's not really my grandmother, by the way, she's my great-aunt. Everyone calls her Granny instead of Grania."

"But I thought, I mean, you being king and all. You seem to belong here. Like the mountain itself."

She blushed, aware that she was painting a romantic picture of him.

He grinned his crooked grin.

"Of course I belong here. This is where my family comes from, generation after generation. These are my 'roots,' as you would say. But I can't make a living here any more than my parents could. I'm not a farmer or a fisherman. We own a holiday resort in Connemara. You know, cottages for tourists. And we do travel packages to archaeological sites. I'm starting a degree in early history at the University of Galway so the two will go together, my studies and the family business. I'll always come back to Inch, and I expect to retire here someday, but my life is elsewhere."

Gwen was struggling to keep her dismay in check.

"What does Granny think of your work?"

"She thinks it's brilliant. I'll be doing something I love. Business is booming with the new currency. Other Europeans can see what they're getting for their money. The more we unite with—"

Dara's excitement died when he caught Gwen's look.

"What on earth is wrong?"

With anyone else she might have hidden it, but with him she couldn't lie or pretend.

"It all sounds so . . . ordinary."

Impatience flickered in his face, then he relented.

"Ach, Gwen! Ireland isn't a fairy tale of wishes and dreams. It's a real place with real people in it. We have to make our living like everyone else in the world."

"But what about your kingship?" she persisted. "And Faerie and the old ways and everything Granny knows?"

He shook his head.

"Why does it always have to be either/or? Mundane or magic? Body or soul? I don't put things into separate boxes. I live with all of it."

Suddenly Gwen understood, not only him but herself

as well. Here was her problem with the fairies in a nut-shell. Either. Or. Practical reality. Airy Fairyland. *She* was the one who made them opposites, and then kept changing her mind about which she preferred. And here were Dara and Granny, comfortable with both, because they did not see the worlds as mutually exclusive.

The two continued up the mountain, talking about their lives, their families, their hopes for the future.

"I've always wanted to be a teacher," she told him. "It's in my blood. Both my parents are, but it's not just that. I love kids. I'm always babysitting, not just for the money but because I like it."

"All the little boys will have crushes on you," he said, laughing.

As the path grew narrower and choked with gorse, they broke apart to walk in single file. From time to time, Dara would go ahead to scout the way. He was much fitter than she. Gwen had already promised herself to join her mother's gym, or maybe jog with her dad. At one point she stopped to catch her breath, and gazed over Lough Swilly. Her heart jumped. She shaded her eyes.

A dark shape was moving over the surface of the lake. A long ragged streak. Was it a bed of floating seaweed? It had to be very large to be visible from that distance. An undertow perhaps? It was advancing swiftly toward the island. The shadow of a cloud? But the sky was almost clear, only faint wisps of cirrus.

She called out to Dara. The wind buffed her words;

he didn't hear them. Quickening her pace, she hurried after him. When she stopped to glance behind her once more, she froze with terror.

The dark shape had reached the shore and was flowing over the sand like an oily slick. Now it slid across the road and onto the trail that led up to the Cairn. It was following in her footsteps! Fear seized her mind, numbing her thoughts, paralyzing her. Even if she had tried, she couldn't move. She was mesmerized like a small creature stalked by a predator.

On the path above, Dara had stopped at a barrier of stinging nettles and turned back for Gwen. Now his cries echoed over the mountainside as he spied her peril.

But she heard nothing. Indeed, she could hardly see what bore down on her as it blotted out the sun and the light of day. Everything in her sight went dim. As the shadow blew its breath upon her, a piercing chill invaded her body. She shivered uncontrollably. Her own breath streamed like gray mist. A thought entered her mind that the sun had never existed, nor had light or warmth. There was nothing but the cold and bitter void.

Now the dark shape opened like a maw to consume her. In its depths she caught a glimpse of a viperous form exuding power and terror. It was only for a moment, but that moment was an eternity, a descent into the abyss where no life existed. Her very soul trembled.

Gwen struggled against the despair that threatened to overwhelm her. Desperately she clung to some faint sense of herself, some feathered memory of light and hope. Alone in the universe, with no one to help her, she fought to hold the darkness at bay.

But she was not alone. Even Dara was not aware of the change that came over him, though he raced recklessly down the path so cautiously climbed just before. For it was not a boy in blue jeans who ran toward her, but a kingly figure trailing a royal mantle.

As soon as he reached Gwen, he stepped in front of her to block the shadow.

"Bí ar shiúl!" he cried, raising his hand. "Be gone from the island! The king commands it!"

The shape loomed larger and darker. Gwen suffered a pang of new fear, not for herself but for Dara. He looked so slight against the shadow, and his voice sounded pale in the dimness. She wanted to help him, or at least to stand by him, but she was rooted to the spot unable to move.

Dara's breath misted in front of him. His body trembled in the icy cold. But he didn't waver. He raised his other hand till both were extended to bar the horror.

"By *Fír Flathemon*, the Sovereign's Truth, I am the law on this island. Even you must obey me!"

And now it appeared Dara was not alone. All around him were shining figures, stern and kingly, called to defend the rights of their lineage. When he spoke again, his voice echoed with theirs, the voices of his ancestors ringing down through the centuries.

"*Gread leat!*" he thundered with inexorable force. "Return to the Deep! The king commands it!"

A great spasm convulsed the shadow. As it backed away, down the path it had come, it slowly diminished like darkness before dawn. By the time it reached the lough, it was a smear of mist that dispersed over the water.

Finally free of the thing's hold, Gwen shuddered behind Dara and covered her face with her hands. He turned quickly to put his arms around her.

"Are you all right?"

Despite the sunlight, she was shivering violently. A film of darkness seemed to linger around her. She struggled to shed it like a skin.

"Was that the fairies?"

"No," he said shortly. "It was something far older. It's what I was afraid of. We must get away from here!"

"But what was it? Do you know?"

"Not here," he urged, catching her hand. "That was only the shadow. Not the thing itself."

He didn't have to say more. Gwen was not only keeping up with him, she was leading the way, pulling at him to make him run faster. One thing she knew, that thing had come for *her*. She never wanted to face it again, or any other version of its horror.

Reaching the road, they ran without stopping till they burst into Granny's.

"The shadow of the Hunter," Dara gasped between breaths. "It came out of the lough!"

The Wise Woman was already nodding before he finished. The remains of her oracle lay on the table—white candles, a scrying glass, quill and ink, and lunar charts marked with calculations.

Granny's voice rang with dread.

"The night of the Hunter's Moon is upon us. The time of the sacrifice."

Twenty-three

G wen felt the chill grip of new fear. Granny sat her down in a chair by the hearth. Dara added more turf to the small fire in the grate. Their simple actions comforted her, but she knew they were preparing to give her bad news. It was Granny who explained.

"Faerie is a wondrous dream, but all things cast a shadow. Even the story of Paradise was wrapped in the snake's tail. Beyond the gates of Faerie lies a mystery in the shape of a Great Worm. Crom Cruac is his name and he is also called the Hunter. Driven from Faerie at the dawn of time, immortal and indestructible, he is bound by a form of tribute.

"At a certain time on the fairy calendar, which may be centuries or more in human terms, a hostage is sacrificed to appease his appetite. If this were not so, he would rise up and devour Faerie itself. Even as the Great Worm exacts a tribute from the fairies, they in turn exact one from us. The sacrifice, the hostage, must come from our race."

"*I, too, was the Hunted and the Sacrificed,*" Gwen murmured.

"There is often danger in entering Faerie," the Wise Woman continued. "But whoever has the misfortune to arrive in the time of the Hunter's Moon faces the greatest peril of all. By a simple stroke of fate, they become the hostage. The sacrifice. I think you know what this means, my dear, though it pains me to tell you."

"Findabhair."

Gwen felt numb. She could hardly think.

"But why did the Hunter come after me? Because I'm her cousin?"

Granny reached out to clasp Gwen's hand.

"Your link to her is one of name and blood, but stronger again is the bond of fairy law. Since the night in the Mound of the Hostages at Tara, the King of Faerie has laid claim to you both. For him, two hostages meant a double-fold gain. One to live as his bride. The other to die as his sacrifice."

"Tricky divil indeed," Gwen said bitterly.

It all made sense now. The unrelenting nature of Finvarra's pursuit. The mounting ferocity of the hunt. Here was the dark plot that Findabhair had suspected, and the source of Midir's concerns. The shadow behind Faerie's glamour. The worm at the heart of the apple. Gwen felt sick. Her triumph over the King could mean only one thing. Findabhair would be the hostage who died as the sacrifice.

Like the flames in the hearth, Gwen's anger rose to thaw her shock.

"I don't accept this. And I don't care if it's tradition or law or what. My cousin is not going to die. Now, more than ever, I've got to get her out of Faerie."

Granny raised her eyebrows. Dara let out a whoop.

"I'm with you, girl! Come hell or high water!"

"Very aptly put," was the old woman's warning. "You mean to defy the fairies, but it may bring the Hunter down upon you."

Gwen shuddered at the thought, but she remained firm.

"I've got to do it."

"Come on, Gran," Dara urged. "You know you're with us. Life's a risk, and you've always taken it."

His great-aunt managed a brief smile, but her look was troubled.

"Here is the brunt of the matter. There is more at stake than we originally feared. If we fail in our challenge to free Findabhair from the fairies, we could lose Gwen as well. You know what that means. She would become the sacrifice."

It was at that moment that Gwen considered retreating. She would never forget her confrontation with the shadow on the mountain. The thought of facing it again—worse, the original of its horror—caused an anguish inside her that was almost unbearable. Her natural instinct for survival warred against her desire to save her cousin. She didn't want to die.

"I'll take the chance," she stated at last.

Dara's look was all the support she needed, but he added words to bolster it.

"It's a gamble, but some of the odds are with us," he said. "We have your arts, Granny, along with my hereditary rights of kingship. And we have Gwen. She has countered every trick and trial the King has set against her so far. It would be wrong to underestimate her now."

Gwen felt a surge of warmth at his praise. At the same time she caught a glimpse of the truth behind his words.

"You speak rightly, Dara," Granny agreed. "We three have power. Though seven is the strongest number, a triad wields great force." She smiled at the two of them with affection and respect. "Oh my dears, this will not be easy, and we may yet fail, but I know in my heart we are right to do it."

They spent the afternoon making their preparations. Once again, the cottage was fortified to bar the fairies. Windows, doors, and all liminal places were wreathed with garlands of elder and broom, and bunches of primroses, heather, holly, and nettle. Once the house was girded, they armed themselves. Granny brandished a staff of blackthorn, her witch's rod. The ogham runes engraved in the wood crawled over its veneer like glittering insects. From an antique chest lined in damask, Dara took out an oaken scepter. It was finely carved with a point like a spear. He slid it into his back pocket as if it were a knife. Only now, when she saw it again, did Gwen remember it from the night of the three sisters.

"It's my badge of office," he told her, "handed down from king to king. In our world it's purely ceremonial. In Faerie, it's a weapon that wields great power."

"I have no magic," Gwen said, with a pang.

"Magic is useless without heart and will," said Granny, "and you have plenty of both. Remember that, even as you use what I am about to give you."

It was a thin wand of hazel, peeled bare and white. As Gwen tucked it into her belt like a dagger, she was told of its nature. Sacred and powerful, the hazel had mystical properties few could plumb. But though she knew little of its spirit, she would be able to wield it if she were brave and true.

At twilight the three set out for Dunfinn, the fairy fort on Inch Island. It was situated on a high promontory in sight of Granny's house. A narrow trail wound up the hill through gorse and wild bramble. The further they went, the more difficult it got. When they reached a sea of bracken as tall as themselves, Granny led the way, using her staff to beat back the greenery. Clouds of midges swarmed in protest. The scent of bruised leaf and stem was suffocating. As the ground grew sodden, the mud sucked at their boots. Nature herself seemed determined to block them. Whenever they reached a patch they couldn't cross—briars like barbed wire, or stinging nettles—they would turn to the left. Deep in thought, each walked in silence, brooding on what might lie ahead.

Their plan was simple, if daring and dangerous. An exchange of hostages. Gwen for Findabhair. Once Findabhair was safe in Granny's cottage, guarded by the Wise Woman, then Gwen would make her move. All being fair in love and war, she would do everything in her power to escape from Faerie. As well as her wits and her hazel wand, she was counting on a little help from her friends. It was Dara's intention to accompany her. As King of Inch, he would claim the right to move freely between the worlds.

"Finvarra may not allow it," Gwen had said, worried.

"He can't keep me out," Dara swore. "There is a tale of an Irish king who dug up a fairy rath to rescue his stolen queen. I'll do the same."

She had no doubt that he would, and it heartened her. Gwen was also expecting some help from Midir, but chose not to mention this to her boyfriend. No need to complicate an already tricky situation. Her fingers curled around the wand at her waist. Regardless of who or what came to her aid, she was ready to fight.

At last they came to Dunfinn. A spinney of straggling hawthorn trees crowned the height. At its center, the ground dipped into a shallow bowl of marsh. An eerie mist whispered through the reeds and rushes. Tall bulrushes stood to attention, a guard of pale spears. It was a forlorn and lonely place, with a strange chill upon it.

Gwen shivered. It was unlike any other spot she had seen on Inch.

"The islanders know this is a fairy fort and they avoid Dunfinn," Dara told her. "But there are plenty of stories about people getting lost on their way home from the pub. After stepping on a *fóidín mearaí*, 'a fairy sod,' they always find themselves here."

"The palace lies beneath," said Granny, "in caverns deep underground. We'll wait till they come for us."

They stood at the edge of the spinney, overlooking the rushes, keeping a watch on Dunfinn. All eyes and ears, they awaited some sign that would herald the approach of the fairy folk: a blast of wind, voices raised in song, or the echo of music. But though the night darkened and clouds drifted past the moon, the silence was unbroken.

"Why do they not come?" Granny said. They could hear the anxiety in her voice. "I sent word of the parley."

"The King doesn't trust us," said Gwen.

"Even if he doesn't," Dara argued, "he'd still come. He'd take the risk. If he loves her, he'll do anything to keep her alive."

Dara was holding Gwen's hand as he said this, and he gripped it tighter.

"He may deceive us in turn," the old woman said suddenly. "There is something in the air. I feel it. Will they try to take Gwen by force?"

The three immediately drew together, back to back.

The shadows in the trees seemed to darken. The night crouched around them, ready to pounce.

"Be of good courage," Granny said softly.

She raised her staff like a spear. Dara took out his scepter and Gwen wielded her wand.

All held their breaths, braced for attack.

The loud crack of a twig made them jump. A slight figure stepped through the trees toward them. Gwen let out a cry.

"Findabhair!"

For there was her cousin, looking pale and calm, dressed in normal clothes, with her knapsack on her back. A quick glance into the spinney confirmed she was alone.

Gwen ran to hug her.

"Thank God you're here! Your life is in danger!"

"If you mean the Hunter's Moon, cuz, I already know." Findabhair's voice was strangely flat. "Finvarra told me himself. He's in love with me and doesn't want me to be the sacrifice."

"So he set you free!" Gwen cried, delighted.

Yet again the King had turned the tables, but this time Gwen didn't mind at all. Breathless with joy, she introduced Findabhair to Dara and Granny, describing how they had come to rescue her.

"You're so American," Findabhair said quietly. "Did I ever ask to be saved?"

Gwen was brought up short by the remark. Dara looked puzzled. But Granny's tone was stern.

"Tell her the truth, girl, or I will. I see the mark on your brow."

Findabhair met the Wise Woman's gaze and recognized another who had lived in Faerie. She bowed her head in acknowledgment, then put her arm around Gwen.

"I've only come back for a little while. To say my good-byes. I'm still the hostage. By my own consent, I will be the sacrifice."

Twenty-four

"Come away from this place," the Wise Woman said quickly.

Findabhair obeyed without protest, even as Dara caught hold of Gwen. Both were hustled from Dunfinn and back to Granny's without a word. But the moment they were safely inside the cottage, Gwen exploded.

"Are you crazy? You're too young to die! And it isn't even your battle! I've put up with your selfishness all through this adventure, off doing your own thing regardless of how it might affect anyone, but this is it! I've had it! I can tell you right now, you're not going to do it. Do you hear me? The word is NO!"

Dara stood in silent support as she wept and raged. Findabhair didn't respond, but hung her head guiltily. When Gwen was finished, pale and shaken, Granny ushered them all to chairs by the fire.

"Why have you chosen to do this, dear one?" she asked of Findabhair, who was slumped in her seat.

"For the sake of Fairyland," came the answer, so quietly spoken it was almost inaudible. "If I don't, they'll all be destroyed, along with Faerie itself. Like the other hostages before me, I go willingly. No mortal has ever been forced."

She leaned toward the flames that were mirrored in her eyes as columns of fire. She had the look of someone newly returned from a foreign land, not fully there. When she was handed a cup of tea, she stared at it awhile before taking a sip, then seemed surprised by the taste. There was something about her that shifted and changed. One moment she was formidable with regal calm and resolve, the next she was trembling, a young girl out of her depth.

"I'm not going alone. Finvarra comes with me. He will abdicate his throne and let Midir rule in his stead. We had a terrible row over it. He wanted to take my place, but I wouldn't allow it. That is my right as the sacrifice. He would do it out of love for me and his kingdom. I do it for the same reason. Don't you see?" She turned suddenly to Gwen, eyes dark with intensity. "It *is* my battle. I am the Faerie Queen."

Gwen's anger dissolved like mist in the sunlight. No matter how much she hated it, she understood the decision. The rescue of Fairyland. It was in all the old tales. Many a human had risked everything to keep that wondrous world alive.

It was an impossible dilemma. How could she condemn her cousin or the Land of Dreams? The death of either was unthinkable.

Gwen sat up suddenly.

"If the hostages have always gone willingly, that means there has never been a fight. Could we challenge Crom Cruac? Save both Findabhair and Faerie?"

Dara let out a low whistle.

"By my kingship, we will try!"

Despite their accord, both were stunned by the immensity of their own proposal. They were further surprised when the Wise Woman concurred.

"All things are possible between heaven and earth," she said slowly, a trace of awe in her voice. "I had a feeling we were heading for something momentous."

The full gist of their talk finally struck Findabhair.

"Are you saying you're willing to go with me and Finvarra? And to fight?" A flush of excitement brought color to her cheeks. For the first time that night she looked her old self. "We need a battle plan!"

"Welcome back, cuz." Gwen grinned. "I missed you."

They all began talking at once, but Granny took command.

"We need a strategy," she agreed, "but if the King has chosen to face Crom Cruac, he should be here with us, to discuss the matter."

"Would he know—" Gwen began.

"He'll know," said Granny and Findabhair together.

There was a moment's silence as old woman and young girl regarded each other.

"Will it be difficult for you?" Findabhair asked quietly.

"No, but what about you?"

"I've never been the jealous sort," the younger said with a shrug. "That's why I get along with them so well."

Only after Finvarra arrived did the others understand the meaning of this exchange.

When the King of Faerie crossed the threshold of the little kitchen, a gust of wind followed, trailing leaves over the floor. It was as if a panther had stalked into the room. Cloaked in black night, glittering with stars, he moved with a languid, powerful grace. In that cozy, very human setting he appeared all the more wild and preternatural.

Instinctively the four humans bowed toward the King. To their surprise, he bowed back.

"Greetings, companions. I come to you most happily. Your decision this night resounds through the halls of Faerie like a call to arms."

He went immediately to Gwen. There was tension in the air as the two faced each other. Her attitude was ambivalent. Once again Finvarra had turned the tables. Despite all that had gone between them, they were now allies in the same cause. But how could she trust him after the things he had done? How could she like him?

Though a faint smile played over the King's lips, his eyes were grave.

"My buttercup has become a mountain rose. A warrior maiden of high courage and strength. It was a game well played, and you won against the odds. It is good, methinks, to have the victor by my side."

She caught her breath. He did it again! His charm had disarmed her.

"I'm glad we're no longer enemies," she said, and she meant it.

"Then I hope we may be friends."

The King addressed Dara next. Laying his hand on the young man's shoulder, he spoke formally.

"Hail, King of Inch. I have known your ancestors, your line is noble. I am glad that you join me on this perilous venture."

Dara replied with equal ceremony.

"All kings and princes look to the High King. It is my duty and honor to stand by you, Sire."

When Finvarra came to Granny, he took her hand and bowed to kiss it. There was a wistfulness to his actions that was also gentle.

"Dear heart, thou art not forgotten. Always my people have watched over you."

"I know that," said the Wise Woman. "And it has meant much to me."

The King's glance rested a moment on her Claddagh ring, which showed two silver hands cupping a heart with a crown.

"You never married? I would not have wished that for you."

"It was my decision," she said firmly. Then a girlish laugh lit up her features. "There was no one who could replace you."

In that moment the others caught a glimpse of an old truth. Granny suddenly appeared as she had in her youth, Grania Harte, a dark-haired beauty who once was consort to the King of the Fairies. Then the image faded and there she stood, gray-haired and aged, yet tall and unbowed.

Lastly, Finvarra came to Findabhair. He didn't touch her, but his very stance was a caress. He inclined toward her like a reed in the wind.

"We need no words, Beloved. Our fates are entwined until the stars fall. It is for you I have taken this path and I do so without regret. Whether fairy or mortal, love is all."

Her empathy with his speech was evident in the light that transformed her. She was no longer a girl but a woman, in the presence of the one she loved and with whom she would willingly die.

Up to that moment Finvarra had been acting in the manner of a High King, with the genteel *courteisie* of the fairy race. Now he dropped his stately pose and stood before them in jeans and black T-shirt. With his dark hair pulled back in a ponytail, he appeared for all the world as a normal if strikingly handsome young man. His eyes were solemn.

"We go as equals, friends, to meet our doom. For no one yet has survived the Hunter's Moon."

Twenty-five

It was late in the night. The hearth fire flickered fitfully as the last flames folded into a labyrinth of red embers. Shadows danced on the walls. Voices murmured in earnest talk. The little group hunched over a mountain of books that spilled from the kitchen table onto the floor. Great tomes bound in leather leaned against volumes of parchment, vellum manuscripts, and modern texts in hardcover and paperback. There were even scrolls of papyrus. The books included grimoires, bestiaries, annals, fables, collections of folk and fairy tales, works of divination and numerology, and ancient histories. Some were gorgeously illuminated with colored inks, while others were so plain and stark they reeked of occult power.

"Every magician's treasure trove," the Wise Woman told them, "is their store of wisdom, their library. Somewhere in these pages lies what we need. Look for items that mention power or battle. Numbers are important. There may even be references to the Worm itself."

"*A cure for chicken pox,*" Gwen read out loud. "*Boil up sheep droppings in a bag in a pot and drink the water.*"

She put the book aside.

"How about this," Findabhair said, grinning. "*A cure for warts: gather stones the number of your warts and throw the stones after a funeral, saying 'Corpse, corpse, carry my warts.'*"

"They worried a lot about warts in the old days," Dara commented. "This book has lashin's about them. Here's a good one. *Take stones for the number of warts, put them in a bag, and leave them by the roadside. Whoever picks up the bag gets your warts.*"

"That's nice," said Gwen.

"We have to sort the wheat from the chaff," the old woman pointed out mildly, "like anything in life."

Gwen threw her cousin a despairing look as Granny produced yet another box from under the stairs. Despite hours of searching, they had yet to find anything.

Findabhair leaned against Finvarra.

"You must know more about this than any book."

He kissed her forehead.

"I know only what has always been known, my love. At the heart of the story about your race and mine is this basic truth: mortals must act to save Faerie. If they do not, we die."

"Here's a number thing," Gwen said suddenly.

The heavy volume was bound with metal clasps, its title was stamped in gilded letters. *The Book of Numbers.* She turned the handwritten pages trimmed with gold leaf. The script was old-fashioned with extravagant flourishes, but it was in English and readable. Each chapter dealt with a number, from one to one thousand, and contained poems, portents, and prophecies.

"Didn't you say seven had the most power?" Gwen asked Granny, as she flipped to the seventh section. She perused the pages quickly. Now her voice shook as she read out loud.

Seven promises are made,
Seven debts will be repaid,
Seven litanies in leaves,
Seven birds and seven sheaves,
Seven yet may herald ruin,
Seven at the Hunter's Moon.

Leaning over her shoulder, Dara was reading ahead on the page. He let out a cry.

"Bigod, here it is! *A charm against the Great Worm!*"

Granny's hands trembled as she took up the book.

"To kill the Worm wherein there is terror, seven angels may do so valiantly."

When no one spoke, Gwen finally asked, "So what does it mean?"

"Our endeavor is possible," Finvarra answered thoughtfully.

Findabhair snorted. "If we find seven angels."

"We've got five right here," was Dara's point. "We'll just have to do it shorthanded."

"NO!" Granny's eyes flashed. She brandished the book as if it were a weapon. "If we are to challenge the universe, we must follow the ancient guides. To do otherwise would be arrogance, the seal of our ruin. If we do not find two more, we act to our peril."

"Two more who believe in fairies in this day and age?" Findabhair spoke bitterly. "And not only that, who love them enough to risk their own lives? We've as much chance as—"

Gwen slapped the table so hard, the others jumped.

"There *are* two more! Right here in Ireland! Two friends of mine! Wow, I can hardly believe this. It's as if—" She stopped. Her face shone with wonder. "This is all meant to happen." She grinned as the others gaped at her. "Well, I can't be a hundred percent sure until I ask them, but I'm pretty certain we've got two more."

The deep frown that furrowed Granny's brow vanished. Her words rang with a confidence that inspired them all.

"Seven were the days of Genesis. Seven are the pillars of life. Seven will be the fires of the Apocalypse. No better number can ride the storm. As a Company of Seven we will forge our destiny."

With Gwen's pledge to summon her friends, the night's deliberations ended. The fire had smoldered into ash. The room was cold. Finvarra glanced out the window with a restless look.

"I can bide here no longer," he said, standing to bow. "Till we meet again, companions."

Findabhair left with him to walk in the garden. The night perfume of trees and flowers scented the air. Moonlight dappled the fields beyond the road. The shadow of the mountains loomed behind them.

"Mortal dwellings are too close for me," said the King.

He was already assuming fairy form, merging with the cloak of night, drifting into the sky brooched with stars.

"Go freely, my love," Findabhair said softly, "till we meet again."

He stooped to kiss her and it was as if the wind caressed her lips, a warm wind but wild too, tasting of earth and leaves and rain-moist air.

When she returned to the house, Gwen met her in the doorway.

"It's impossible," Findabhair said, her eyes wet.

Gwen gave her a hug.

"Nothing's impossible, cuz. After all we've been through, you should know that by now."

Dara had taken the daybed in the kitchen, leaving his room for the girls. The cousins settled down for the night, but with no intentions of sleeping. Despite the late hour they talked till it was almost dawn. There was so much to say, not only of the trial that lay ahead but of the adventures each had had when they were apart.

"I am really and truly sorry," Findabhair said, when she heard Gwen's story. "What a wagon I've been! I got so caught up with Finvarra I hadn't a thought for you, or anything else for that matter. I used to hate girls who dropped their pals because of some boy. But now I know what being madly in love can do to you. Were you furious with me? I wouldn't blame you."

"Funny thing about that. I was and I wasn't. Once I got over the shock of being on my own, and got the hang of doing things for myself, it was really great. If you had been there, I would have been following you around like a dope as usual. And another thing," she added, in a moment of total honesty, "I was really glad you weren't here when I met Dara."

"Oh God, yes, what a sweetie. We would have been tearing out each other's hair for him."

They muffled their laughter under the blankets.

"Is he your boyfriend?"

"Yes," said Gwen. "So keep your eyes and your hands off him."

More giggles. Then Findabhair sighed with envy.

"You're the lucky one. At least he's in the same world as you."

"Oh yeah, sure, like I live in Ireland. You and I are both in for long-distance relationships."

They sighed together.

"And who knows if we'll even have that by the time this is over," Findabhair said gravely.

Gwen shook her head.

"Call me Scarlett, but I'm not going to think about that till tomorrow."

Though her cousin eventually fell asleep, Gwen stayed awake. Light seeped through the curtains and into the room. It seemed to bring the glimmer of promise. A nameless thrill coursed through Gwen. She knew something wonderful was about to happen.

The moment the tapping on the windowpane began, she was up in an instant.

Padding barefoot from the room, in the long T-shirt she wore to bed, Gwen left the cottage. The morning was pale with early sunlight and mist. The grass was cool beneath her feet. A soft breeze played in her hair. Moving instinctively, as if beckoned to follow, she walked around to the back of the house. There Granny's wild garden trailed into a thicket of old oak and holly. On the threshold of the wood stood a tall rowan tree.

Laughter bubbled from Gwen's lips. Her childhood dream come true! Fairies at the bottom of the garden!

It was just as she had always imagined. They bedecked the tree like a mass of bright berries. Tiny and winged, clothed in thistledown and spiderweb, golden-haired, silver-eyed, they glittered like fireflies. Some were asleep, tucked under the leaves. Others flitted in the branches like jeweled hummingbirds. A few shivered as they shyly acknowledged her gaze. Their size took nothing from the wonder of their creation. Does the speck of a star diminish its beauty? Indeed Gwen regarded this cluster of fairies with the same awe she viewed the constellations of heaven. *As above, so below.* Here was life's mystery in all its splendor.

"Thank you," she whispered, with tears in her eyes.

She knew who had sent this precious gift. After all the hardship he had caused her, Gwen was now reconciled with the King of Faerie.

Twenty-six

Katie Quirke strapped the last of her luggage onto the motorbike. Her mother and sisters hovered nearby, waiting to see her off. All were agreed that she deserved this holiday, and they kept repeating their assurances that they could run the farm without her. One last time Katie ran through instructions about certain lambs and calves. One last time she clung to her mother, whose own tears had begun to fall.

"Enough of this nonsense, girl," Mrs. Quirke said gruffly. "You're well overdue a break. You just forget about us and enjoy yourself, do you hear?"

Katie made an effort to control herself, but she couldn't help wondering if she would ever see them again. From Gwen's phone call she knew the nature of the mission, knew that it was dangerous and its outcome uncertain. And yet, though it made this parting painful, wild horses couldn't have kept her away.

The sky had darkened with the threat of rain. Katie

donned her great yellow mack, and eased her helmet over her head. As if girded for battle, she mounted the bike. Waving her last good-byes, she sped down the road and out of the Burren, on the first lap of her journey north.

She was driving through the town of Kilcolgan when she spotted the Mercedes. As the big car overtook her, a shaft of sunlight struck its silver-gray roof with a flash of light. Instinctively Katie raised her hand to salute the driver. More than an hour later, as she left Claremorris, the same car passed her again with a friendly beep. She had already decided to stop for lunch in Sligo, when she spotted the Mercedes parked in front of a hotel. On an impulse, she drew up her bike and went in search of the car's owner.

The hotel was softly lit and plushy, with a long hall-way leading to a spacious lounge. The mahogany tables gleamed with polish, partnered by cushioned stools and chairs. Scenes of the Hunt adorned the walls with hunts-men in red coats, brindled horses and hounds, and the lit-tle rust-colored fox running for its life. Lunch was being served from a carvery bar. The smell of roast beef thick-ened the air. The rattle of cutlery on china countered the noise of piped music.

Katie scanned the crowd. Though she had no idea what the driver looked like, she hoped he would recog-nize her mack and the helmet under her arm. When a stocky red-haired man in a business suit signaled to her, she hurried to join him.

"This is a wild but educated guess," she said. "Are you Mattie O'Shea?"

"Katie Quirke, I presume?"

He put out his hand. The two redheads grinned at each other with instant liking.

"I had hoped you would see the car, and ordered us some lunch," he told her. "Plenty of sandwiches—rounds of beef, ham, and salad—and the soup of the day. Is that all right with you?"

"God bless you, I'm famished! I could eat the leg of a table."

She pulled off her mack and eyed the bar.

"Will you take a drink?" she asked him.

He hesitated a moment.

"You did lunch . . ."

"Right," he agreed. "Pint of Guinness."

When Katie returned with two pints of black stout, they lifted their glasses together.

"*Sláinte.*"

"To the high road and beyond."

"Gwen told me you offered a lift," Katie said, after she took a long sup. "But I prefer to travel on my own steam. And I wanted time to think. No offense?"

"Not at'all," said Mattie. "It worked out for the best. I had a few matters to clear up, just in case." He paused, as a shadow crossed his features, then he steadied himself. "Do you know, when I passed you near Galway, I knew it was you. For a moment, I saw something else. Not a girl on a motorbike, but a giantess on a horse!"

He blushed, as redheads are wont to do, and was about to apologize for talking nonsense.

"I know what you mean," Katie assured him. "Do you know why I waved? When the sun shone on your car, it suddenly looked like a silver chariot. Strange doings are afoot and we are a part of them."

They sat in breathless silence, acknowledging the momentous nature of their journey and the great mystery that awaited them.

"Gwen told me you have a wife and baby? It must have been a hard decision for you."

Mattie sighed heavily. "It was. But I had a long talk with Miriam, and she agrees with what I'm doing. We both come from villages where the old ways haven't died out altogether. It seems right to go when you are called. What about you?"

"I lied." Katie looked shamefaced. "Officially I'm on holidays. My family have enough on their plates with my Da ill and the farm to look after. I'm worried myself about what might happen, but that wouldn't stop me. I feel as if my whole life has been leading to this. I even managed to quit smoking at last, to purify myself in a way. Does that sound daft?"

"Not to me," said Mattie. His middle-aged features were suddenly youthful as the imaginative boy inside him crowed with delight.

When they left the hotel, the two parted as friends.

"*Slán go fóill!*"

"Safe journey till we meet again on Inch!"

—✲   ✲—

When the sleek silver car pulled up outside Granny's cottage, Gwen ran to greet Mattie. The others were a little surprised by his professional appearance, but it wasn't long before he was ensconced in the kitchen, talking and laughing with the rest of them.

It was a good while later, when they were finishing supper, that Katie arrived. Her motorcycle belched a cloud of black smoke as it came to a halt with a sputter. Again Gwen ran out to meet her friend. This reunion was louder, as they hugged with shouts of glee.

"I was in a fit I wouldn't make it!" Katie cried. "Bloody potholes! The exhaust is broken and maybe more. But even if the blasted thing burst asunder I would have come—on foot, if I had to!"

Helmet under her arm, she marched into the house where she greeted Mattie like a long-lost brother. Then she shook hands with Granny, Dara, and Findabhair, pumping their arms with a firm grip. All were impressed by her boundless energy.

"Are you hungry, my dear?" the old woman asked. "I've kept your dinner in the oven."

"God bless you!"

The others dished out their dessert of stewed rhubarb

with custard, while Katie started on her plate of corned beef with cabbage and floury potatoes. The talk around the table flowed freely, punctuated with laughter. It was as if there were no strangers present. As the personalities blended together, each was overcome by the sense they had all met before. In other times and other places, this group had gathered. *As it was, so would it be, now and always.*

"Are we all here?" Mattie asked, looking around. "I have a feeling that someone is missing. As if I'm holding a meeting and my top salesman is absent."

"You too?" Katie exclaimed. "I was thinking, myself, the count was wrong." She started to laugh. "A head short of the herd."

Pleased that the circle was bonding so well, Gwen knew the time had come. She cleared her throat.

"There was something I left out in the phone calls. As you've guessed yourselves, there is another with us. I thought it might be a bit too much to give you the whole story in one go."

Katie caught her breath with a thrill of premonition. She knew Gwen was about to say something wonderful.

"The King of the Fairies is in this with us."

Katie released her breath in a whistle. Mattie looked shaken.

"That's it!" cried Katie. "I'll die happy."

"Let's hope we won't have to," Findabhair warned.

Mattie could barely contain his excitement. His boyhood wish was about to be fulfilled.

"When will he join us?"

"He has asked us to meet him tonight at Inch Castle," said Gwen.

"It's an empty ruin," Dara explained, "but he's uncomfortable in houses."

"A midnight court?" Katie asked, overjoyed.

"A Council of War," was the sobering reply.

Twenty-seven

Shortly before midnight they set out for Inch Castle in Mattie's car. Granny sat in the front passenger seat, while the four young people climbed into the back.

"You'll have to sit on my lap," Dara said, pulling Gwen on top of him.

"There's plenty of room," she protested mildly.

"No there isn't."

He held her firmly and nuzzled her neck.

"I'm being *curcudgellach*," he said.

"What?"

"It's an old Donegal word for 'affectionate.'"

She laughed. "I like it."

Findabhair rolled her eyes at Katie, who was already grinning.

"Everyone comfortable back there?" Mattie asked.

"Some more than others," was Findabhair's response.

At Granny's direction, Mattie drove to the far side of the island. Leaving the main road, he turned up a narrow lane. It took them through a farmyard where they woke the dogs sleeping in the barn. By the time the farmer had opened his window to investigate, the silver car had passed on.

Eventually the lane stopped at a cattle gate that led into a broad field.

"End of the road," Mattie announced. "From here we walk."

They had no difficulty crossing the meadow. Cropped short by sheep, the grass was a trim lawn that shone in the moonlight. The ground rolled downward to a rocky shore that met the restless waters of Lough Swilly. And there on the rocks, like a great broken tooth, jutted the ruin of Inch Castle.

It had been abandoned for centuries. Empty windows stared blindly over field and lough. The shattered walls were clotted with ivy. A cold mist snaked through the rubble of stones.

As the group made their way toward the castle, Dara told the most notorious tale of its history.

"In the great days of O'Doherty rule, Inch was the richest territory in Inishowen. In the fifteenth century, two cousins called Donnell and Rory fought for its sovereignty. One imprisoned the other in the castle and set it ablaze. The victim, Donnell, broke free somehow and came out on the battlements. Rory was camped below in this very field. Maddened with rage, Donnell tore a great stone from the ramparts and hurled it down on top of his cousin. Needless to say, Donnell claimed the kingship."

"God, what a story," said Katie. "Those ancient lads were pure wild!"

She had no sooner spoken than the air resounded with the clash of metal. Inch Castle began to waver. Then all of them saw the scene. Flames shot out from the windows, burning the sky with a bloodred glow. Men thronged the field below, weapons gray and glinting. A figure high on the walls, furious and roaring, lifted a huge boulder over his head.

"Look away!" Granny said quickly. "Stop thinking about it! Time and space go awry near the fey folk."

Even as they obeyed her the din of war receded, and the ghosts of the past dispelled like mist. But the castle did not return to ruins. Rather, it stood now as it had in its heyday.

Fully restored, finely pointed and mortared, the walls rose up to challenge the sky. Present also were the wings and buttresses that had long since fallen into the lough. Tasseled banners fluttered above the turrets. The citadel was ablaze with light. Chandeliers could be seen through vaulted arches, flickering with the lights of a thousand candles. From the tall lancet windows music issued forth.

The group quickened their pace. They knew what this meant. Fairy revels were taking place within.

As soon as they reached the oaken door of the castle, it swung open before them. Riotous sounds rushed out to greet them. They stepped over the threshold and into a fairy tale.

In the blink of an eye, each was arrayed in shining garments. Katie was resplendent in froths of yellow muslin, with her shoulders bared and her hair caught up in golden combs. Granny was a stately matron in silver-gray silk with a long white train hemmed with diamonds. Gwen twirled with delight in a rose-colored gown embroidered all over with wild red roses. Rubies dripped from her ears and throat. Findabhair's beauty was accented once again in her favorite black, a sheen of ebony stippled with pearls.

The men were handsome in bright linen tunics with cloaks tossed dashingly over one shoulder. Dara was in scarlet, like the famous Pimpernel, with a dark mantle fringed with gold. Mattie wore various hues of forest-green and his cloak was clasped with a brooch of emeralds. On his head was a jaunty plumed hat.

The hall itself was dressed for fun and frolic. Tables groaned under the weight of a fabulous feast, sweetmeats and savories and mouthwatering confections. Marble fountains dispensed spiced wines, warm reds and cool whites. Champagne bubbled like mountain springs. The air reverberated with tumultuous tunes, as the assembly capered on deft feet without stopping for breath.

"Council of War?" Gwen said, laughing.

"The fairy way." Findabhair grinned. "Party first, work later."

"Proper order," Katie declared, looking around with satisfaction. "A taste of what I'm fighting for."

There was no more time for talk. The fairy folk came running to draw them into the festivities, and their company was scattered throughout the hall.

"It's yourself, no less!" came a shout behind Gwen.

Recognizing the voice, she whirled around to face the leprechaun. Her jaw dropped as she took in his outfit.

Fancifully dressed in a green suit with tails and a vest of gold brocade, he wore a magnificent top hat crowned with shamrocks. His feet were shod with black patent shoes clasped with silver buckles.

"Why waste a perfectly good stereotype," he said, in response to her look. "I hear you've been havin' a grand oul time in me absence. Fair play to ye! How about a dance?"

Before she could resist, he clutched her around the waist and dragged her onto the floor.

"Ouch!" she said, as he trod on her toes.

"Asha, don't I have two left feet?"

She looked down, and sure enough he did! She was wondering frantically how she could escape, when Midir cut in.

Dressed in a dark-blue tunic with a silver cloak, he twirled her away.

"Have I saved a damsel in distress?"

"My champion," she said, laughing. "You're always rescuing me."

"It is my pleasure."

She was still with Midir by the time Dara caught up

with her to claim a dance. The red-haired *Tánaiste* yielded his partner, but not without reluctance.

"I think he fancies you," Dara said, as they waltzed away.

"As a matter of fact," Gwen replied airily, "he does."

A furrow of jealousy creased Dara's brow.

Gwen started to laugh.

"Men are so ridiculous. Always forgetting the important question. Who do I like?"

Dara laughed too, and drew her closer.

"Don't you mean who do you *love*?"

"Maybe."

Yes, she had definitely become a flirt.

"Let's get stuck into the feast," Dara suggested, looking over at the banquet table.

Gwen let go of his hand.

"Don't you remember what I told you?" she said, wincing. "How I failed that test?"

"You and God-knows-how-many others. According to Granny, who failed it too, you'd have to *hate* food to pass it."

"That wouldn't be me," Gwen said ruefully. Then she brightened as the truth struck home. "And you know what? I like being me. To hell with diets. Where's that chocolate mousse?"

It was sometime later that Midir discovered Katie, and the two redheads spun onto the floor with wild abandon.

"This is the life!" cried Katie, as the hall whirled around her.

"It could be yours, if you wish."

"Go 'way with you. You're sweeping me off my feet."

Mattie wouldn't dance at first, despite the entreaties of the beautiful fairy women. He stood at the edges of the throng, gazing in quiet bliss like one enchanted.

The fairies murmured among themselves.

"Will our guest not dance?"

"He will, he will. She's on her way."

"Has the King sent for her?"

"Of course. You'll see."

Though Mattie overheard them, he didn't understand their words until he saw her. She moved through the crowd as gracefully as a swan. Clad in a gown of red satin with diamonds in her hair, she looked beautiful and vivacious.

"Miriam! What on earth—"

He ran to embrace her but stopped, overcome with awe, even as he had been when he first courted her. Removing his plumed hat with a flourish, he bowed before her.

"Matt, is this a dream? Or are we really in Fairyland?"

"I think the answer is yes to both, my love. Shall we dance?"

Granny, too, was drawn onto the floor, for in Faerie no limbs are old or weary. Fond cries met her on all sides —"Grania, you have returned to us!"—as the fairies greeted a former queen.

It was the same for Findabhair, their present queen.

Wherever she walked they gathered around her, kissing her hand, and murmuring their gratitude. For they knew the choice she had made on their behalf. She was touched by their affection, but her eyes kept searching the hall. Though she was accustomed to fairy protocols and knew Finvarra would be late, she couldn't enjoy herself until he arrived.

Wandering away from the crowd, she stood alone in an alcove overlooking Lough Swilly. The moon was mirrored in the water, rippling on the waves. It was like a pale-gold creature, precious and fragile, asleep below the surface. In the distance, dark mountains kept watch like sentinels.

"I wish this would stop," she sighed.

His absence was like an itch she couldn't scratch, an ache she couldn't soothe. Food tasted bland, music sounded dull, and colors looked gray. Life without him was a shadow. She had never felt this way before. The depth of her emotions was disturbing. Things were out of control and there was nothing she could do about it.

"It is no easier for me, Beloved," he murmured behind her.

Finvarra's arms encircled her as he lay his head on her shoulder.

Findabhair turned to embrace him.

The King's sloe-black eyes brooded upon her.

"Since time began I have loved freely, never losing myself utterly in any one woman. You have disrupted my life as greatly as I have yours."

"Is that supposed to make me feel better?" she said, though of course it did.

He saw this and his humor lightened.

"It was your name that first drew me to you, my sweet Findabhair. So like to mine and no others bear it. I should have been warned instead of drawn. It is doom to meet one's equal."

Findabhair laughed. The King grasped her tighter to show how meaningless were his words.

"I missed you," she said.

"Only three days, *a stór*, and did I not come to you each night?"

"That was really you? I thought it was only my dreams."

"Dreams are never 'only,'" he chided. "But come, my Queen. It is not love but war that we must look to this night."

They stepped out from the alcove, one human, one immortal, both clothed in night's black and arrayed with stars. As they walked arm-in-arm toward the assembly, the music and dancing ceased and trumpets blared out.

"Make way for Their Majesties! Make way for the King and Queen of Faerie!"

Twenty-eight

From their various corners of the hall, the others came to meet the King. Finvarra greeted them warmly, especially the newcomers whom Gwen presented.

"Dearest Caitlín," he said to Katie, kissing her hand. "The finest woman that ever went in the walls of a farm." She colored with pleasure, for he used a Burren expression to honor her. "Have we mended your walls well? Have we kept guard over your herds?"

"Your people have always been good to me, Sire."

"And you have always been a good neighbor to us."

He caught a stray tress of her red hair and tucked it back into place.

"You put me in mind of my *Tánaiste*. Perhaps one day, my sweet, you will tire of mortal toil and join him in Faerie."

Katie's eyebrows shot up like two birds leaving the branch.

"Something to think about when the going gets rough," the King whispered in her ear.

"Hail, Maitiú," he said, turning to Mattie who was holding his wife's hand. "Your family are known to me from past generations. Your great-grandfather once stood before me, even as you do now. Did he keep the piece of gold he won from me in the wager over a hare and a tortoise?"

Mattie's eyes widened.

"So that old tale was true! My granny always maintained he had drink taken that night, but no one could explain the beautiful coin. It was passed down to me. I have always cherished it."

The King of Faerie smiled.

"You have kept faith with us, despite modern disbelief. A brave stance for a man of business."

Mattie squared his shoulders.

"Some old beliefs hold up progress, but there's no point in throwing out the baby with the bathwater. Why go blindly into the future with nothing at our back?"

"Spoken like a champion!" Finvarra declared.

"And good evening to you, *mo chara*," he said to Miriam, who curtsied before him. "Have you enjoyed my feast?"

"Very much, sir, thank you," she said. Then her smile wavered. "But I think I know why you invited me."

There was sorrow in his eyes as he acknowledged her intuition.

"It was not an easy thing you did when you gave your husband leave to answer our call. We are most grateful. I will do whatever is in my power to ensure this is not a final parting."

Miriam stiffened suddenly and turned to her husband.

"The baby's crying. I must go. You are in good company, my dearest. I can only hope and pray that they will bring you back to me."

Mattie kissed his wife even as she faded away, returning to her bed where she woke at the sound of a child's cry.

"Now, friends," the King announced, "it is time we held our Council. A room has been prepared."

They followed him up a winding staircase into a great chamber at the top of the castle. It was a stern and spartan hall hung with weapons from every age. Tapestries depicted ancient battles. The fireplace burned whole logs. Vaulted windows looked out over the ramparts to the misty mountains. In the center of the room, flanked by high-backed chairs, was a table as round as the moon.

"Like King Arthur's!" Gwen cried, delighted.

"As with his court," said Finvarra, "we are a company of equals. "

When all were seated, a solemn air fell over them. Granny, as Wise Woman, rose to address the gathering.

"This is a Council of War. We are agreed that we will defy Crom Cruac. What remains to be decided is how and when. We'll begin with the how of it. Finvarra?"

"There are two gates to Faerie," the King told them, "which mark the borders of our territory in time, though not in space. The White Gates of Morning are the entrance to Faerie. The Black Gates of Night are the exit. It is in the chasm beyond the Gates of Night that Crom Cruac lies. On the night of the sacrifice, the hostage passes through the gates. Once they go beyond we know naught what befalls them."

Findabhair shuddered, then took comfort as she looked around at her friends.

"Crom Cruac is called 'the Great Worm.' Do we know anything else about him?" asked Katie. She wanted to know the worst, to be ready for it.

Once again Finvarra answered.

"I cannot recall a time when he did not exist. Yet, it must be said, my people were young and unknowing in the early days of the world. Our memories of that time are as dim as your own childhoods. This I do know. It was not Faerie that expelled Crom Cruac beyond our gates, though mortal tales would have it so. According to our own legends, he was chained there by the Archangels after a great war in the Empyrean, a realm higher than our own."

"Oh God, I hope he isn't who I think he is," Katie muttered. "I haven't been to Mass in ages."

Mattie was thinking along the same lines. Only now was he considering the true nature of the beast. Though he had no intentions of turning back, he couldn't help but ask.

"Do we dare?"

The Wise Woman's look was sympathetic, but her voice was firm.

"The mouse may look upon the cobra. The hare upon the hawk. There is no law in the universe that forbids this."

As the company absorbed her words, each faced the bottom line.

"You mean we have the right to die trying," Dara said.

A silence fell till Findabhair spoke up.

"We may not die!" she avowed. "It could be *his* destiny to die at this time and ours to do the deed."

"Well said, my Queen," Finvarra saluted her.

They sat tall in their chairs, like lords and ladies. The ghosts of old battles whispered from the tapestries. Camlann. Clontarf. The Fields of Culloden. The shadows of lost and noble causes. For better or worse, some wars had to be fought.

"So be it," Granny concluded. "Together we go beyond the Gates, to meet our destiny. There is only one question left. When?"

"Crom Cruac chooses the time of the sacrifice," Finvarra said. "It is our custom to await his summons."

"I'd rather not wait, thanks," said Katie.

"We should attack beforehand," Mattie agreed. "Catch him off guard and possibly weaker."

Dara nodded. "We're already breaking the rules. Why keep to an appointed time?"

Excitement rippled around the table as they all concurred.

"My former adversary has yet to speak," Finvarra said. He regarded Gwen curiously. "What says the Captain of our company?"

There was no humor or irony in the King's words. He was evidently serious about the title he gave her. Gwen felt a flutter of panic. She tamped it down. Indeed. Wasn't she the one who had brought them all together? Wasn't it her decision to fight against the Hunter's Moon? She *was* the Captain of the Company of Seven.

She had remained quiet throughout the Council, studying the group, noting their strength and courage. Their morale was at its peak after the fairy feast. Like warriors of old who had been feted before battle, their spirits were high. She could feel the power in the circle. Newly joined together, they were at their best, before minor differences could weaken their unity.

She knew that what she was about to propose hadn't occurred to any of them yet. But both logic and instinct told her it was right. She took a deep breath, and stood up.

"We go tonight. Not later, but this very minute."

It was as if a thunderclap had struck the room. They jumped to their feet, propelled by the truth. There were no preparations to make. There was no reason to delay.

The night of the Hunter's Moon had come.

Twenty-nine

I nch Castle was a dark and empty ruin once more. The Company of Seven stood alone outside the walls. The night was somber, barely lit by a pallid moon. The cold waters of Lough Swilly lapped against the shore. A gray mist straggled over the ground. In the distance a dog barked. The humans in the Company drank in this moment, aware they might never see their world again. The fairy glamour was gone. Their own clothes had returned, bringing with them a sense of vulnerability.

"It's all so sudden," Findabhair said quietly. "It changes everything."

"Yeah," Gwen sighed. "My crummy old life doesn't look half-bad after all." She glanced at Dara. "And just when things were getting good."

His jaw was clenched, the only sign he was anxious. As she leaned against him, he took her hand.

"I've never felt less like a king," he admitted. He gave her a long look. "I wish we'd had more time together."

"Me too."

It was one of those moments when everyone felt extremely fond of one another. They were courteous, even shy, as they exchanged last words and embraces.

"You're the best friend I've ever had," Findabhair said to her cousin. "Sorry for being such a bollocks."

"Hang in there, cuz. Last one home's a pumpkin."

Saluting Gwen, Mattie grinned his encouragement.

"Oh captain, my captain."

And Katie gave her a big hug.

"I knew we'd be friends till the end. I just didn't think it would come so soon!"

"This isn't the end," Gwen insisted, though she was less sure than she sounded.

"Courage, noble hearts," Granny said quietly. "We are not alone. Faerie will strengthen us before we go, for we must cross the Blessed Realm to reach Crom Cruac."

Finvarra inclined his head in agreement. Catching Findabhair's hand, he led them to a grassy mound not far from the castle. As they drew closer, they saw the door in the hill. The archway was fashioned of two standing stones with a lintel stone overhead. It was covered with spiral motifs; some were like whorled eyes and others like snakes swallowing their own tails.

Granny studied the carvings.

"Ouroboros?" she murmured.

"There are many entrances to Faerie," Finvarra told them, "but my people favor these tumuli which have the nature of thresholds. Let us begin our journey."

He passed through the archway, with Findabhair close behind. One by one, each followed after. There was a moment when the stones seemed to close in on them, and each felt enclosed in a tomb that smelled of dank earth. Then with a final push, like life, like death, they came out on the other side.

"Open one door and you find another," the King said, when all had passed through.

They stood in a milky void, as if inside a cloud. Towering before them was a gigantic white gate. The railings shone of pale alabaster, the great fluted arch was inlaid with ivory. The portcullis, which had begun to rise, had the silvery sheen of mother-of-pearl.

"The pearly gates?" asked Gwen, surprised.

Finvarra smiled.

"Some mortal once glimpsed it and thought it so, the Gates of Heaven, but it is the White Gates of Morning that lead to my realm."

Whether it took seconds or aeons to cross that beautiful kingdom, they couldn't know. Time meant nothing in a land suspended between morning and night, for it held the breadth of infinity within its borders. And whether the countryside swept past them like wind, or they traveled themselves at impossible speeds, they couldn't be sure. For it seemed they were given hinds' feet as they leaped over mountains, vast plains, and boundless seas. Everything shone with a startling clarity of light, an eternal summer's day. *For lo, the winter is*

past, the flowers appear on the earth, and the time of the
singing of birds is come.

Tír Tairngire. Land of Promise. *Magh Abhlach.* Plain of
the Apple Trees. *Tír na nÓg.* Kingdom of the Forever-
Young. It was a country that refreshed the spirits of all who
journeyed there, delighting the mind and nourishing the
soul. The fair flowering place where there is no grief or sickness or death. The many-colored land of dreams and
enchantment. The far green country under a swift sunrise.

They sailed like birds on currents of air spiced with
perfumes. *Spikenard and saffron, calamus, and cinnamon,
with all trees of frankincense, myrrh, and aloes.* They
swam like sea creatures in the Land Below the Waves.
When they ate of the fruit in an orchard of pomegranates,
the fiery seeds burst on their tongues like cool flame. *A
fountain of gardens. A well of living waters.* From every
corner resounded sweet strains and airs, the music of the
spheres, the song of forever.

Only when they neared the end of their journey did
they become aware of the changes that had been wrought
upon them. As if they had passed through the waters of
rebirth, or the purifying rite of a baptismal fire, each was
transformed. They displayed the aspect of what they *might*
be, no longer on the inside but shining without. Like a
radiant garment, they wore the form that was their soul.

In a white-and-gold gown woven with the signs of the
zodiac, Granny reflected the wisdom of the ages. Two
ivory horns upon her headdress clasped a golden disc that

was the full moon. A silver serpent twined around her staff. She was the High Priestess.

Dara stood with commanding majesty, in a tunic of royal purple with a gold-fringed cloak. At his side hung the archetypal sword. His shield was emblazoned with the mark of the pendragon. His crown was engraved with interlocking oak leaves, for he was Daire, the Oak King.

At Dara's right hand stood Mattie, the boar lord of the warrior band, the battering ram, the fury of battle. His shield was of black alder embossed with metal knobs. He gripped a lance that challenged the sky. His stance bespoke the indomitable pride of his ancestry, Champion of the Gael.

How would Finvarra be enhanced? What could be brighter than the King of Faerie? In chain mail of woven light, he carried a golden sword and spear. From his shoulders unfurled two massive wings; not the gossamer appendages his race sported at times, but the swan's span of feathered strength, ribbed with iron bone and muscle. He had become his higher self, the avenging Archangel.

The three young women bore the three faces of the Goddess.

Clothed in forest-green, Katie gripped the arc of a great bow in her hands. Over her shoulder was slung a quiver of arrows. Her burnt-red hair was pulled back to reveal a cool brow. She was the woman who needed no man, for she was strength and prowess herself, the Huntress.

Findabhair was aglow in sunset colors, the ardent

hues of the Goddess of Love. But she did not express love's playful nature, nor its serenity. She exuded passion, the kind that shatters all order and bring empires to their knees. She carried two swords, one in each hand, for love can be double-edged and deadly.

Gwen thought herself the most changed among them, though her friends did not agree. A heavy green mantle fell from her shoulders, and a golden torc ringed her throat. At her back hung a shield, round as the sun. In one hand she grasped a spear, while the wrist of the other held a hooded white falcon. Wild courage coursed through her veins. For she was a braveheart, a trueheart, the Celtic Warrior-Queen.

Thus arrayed in the blessings of the Land of Ideals, the Company of Seven arrived at their destination. The place of their destiny.

To kill a worm wherein there is terror, seven angels from Paradise may do so valiantly.

As colossal as the portal that had granted them entrance, the Black Gates of Night loomed, the final exit. The dark gleam of ebony and obsidian sent a cold chill through them. All were suddenly filled with dread, for they heard the whisper in the deepest recesses of their minds.

Abandon hope, all ye who enter here.

Thirty

After journeying through eternal day, they came to an abyss of endless night. No moon had ever glimmered here. No sun had ever risen to warm these shadows. Cheerless it was, with a cruel chill and the pall of darkness. Inchoate shapes moved in the gloom, taking form for a moment and then dissolving again. Nothing was solid or permanent. Bewildered, the Company put words on the landscape in an effort to understand. The sullen contours in the distance were a range of mountains. The ground underfoot was a rocky shore. Before them lay a tarn of black water.

Whatever they named in their minds came into being and petrified, but there was no joy in the naming or in what it created. The lack of light and warmth was almost unbearable. The cold seeped into their bones with a groping horror.

For the six humans, this was an encounter with the deepest nightmare of their race. It was as if they had awakened in the dead of night to hear the pitiless secret uttered. *At the heart of life is a void without purpose or meaning. There is no God. There is no love. All is emptiness and loneliness. Since time began, you have been abandoned.*

Even Finvarra was shaken. King of a bright country, he had always viewed night as a time for sport and play. But there were no bonfires here to encourage a dance, no stars to smile on merry capers, no nocturnal creatures calling him to join their revels. This dark land knew nothing of pleasure.

For Gwen, the place was especially disturbing. She recognized the deathly cold that clutched at her heart, the breath of the thing that had come out of the lough. But there was no sign of the shadow, nor of the viperous terror she had glimpsed in its depths. There was nothing here but desolation.

Is this the battle? she wondered to herself. Do we create the enemy? Is it a thing of the mind?

Thinking along the same lines, Granny spoke out loud.

"Perhaps the true test is to keep faith in the dark."

Her words broke the silence, like a stone dropped into a well. A tremor shook the still weight of the water, as if something below shuddered awake. Ripples crossed the oily surface. A bubbling sound could be heard. The agitation increased, till waves slapped ominously at the shore where they stood.

As the lake convulsed, the Company felt its upheaval in the depths of their minds. *Something wicked this way comes.* A nameless terror seized them. They hardly dared to breathe. The suspense was torment in itself.

But they didn't have long to wait.

Like the kraken from the deep, the Great Worm rose up with an eerie silence more dreadful than a scream. He was darker than the night itself. A thousand eyes glared from his body. Gargantuan and glittering, like a spray of cold stars, he appeared to have no head, no tail, no beginning or end. Crom Cruac, the Hunter.

Each of the Company felt the bane of his stare. Merciless eyes pierced their being, burning their souls, reducing them to ashes. He saw all, knew all, extinguished all.

And they sensed what he saw as he beheld them: seven specks of light besieged by darkness.

Though he had no mouth, a fell voice resounded in their thoughts.

Why come you here?

Stunned by his presence, by a titanic reality they could barely grasp, no one responded at first.

Then Findabhair found the will to speak. Her words quivered, small and pale in the dark.

"I am the hostage of the Hunter's Moon."

The others immediately closed ranks around her.

I have not called you, but I acknowledge your existence. Do you consent to be the sacrifice?

Before Findabhair could answer, her friends cried out.

"SHE DOES NOT!"

The disturbance in Crom Cruac shook the very foundations of the world. The ground quaked beneath them. The dark tarn seethed and boiled like a cauldron. The distant mountains began to erupt, spewing fire into the sky with billows of black smoke.

You dare to break a timeless covenant.

They didn't wait for his attack, but moved instinctively to fight for their lives.

Experienced in battle, Finvarra led the charge. He flew on mighty wings toward the Worm, his sword flashing with light. The rest followed, drawing their weapons as they ran.

Katie scaled a height of rocks nearby and took up position. Silver streaked through the air as she let fly her arrows. The others bore down on the Worm with sword and spear.

Only to find their blades rebound as if his skin were armored.

"The eyes!" cried Mattie. "Go for the eyes!"

Indeed they were the only penetrable area. Spears pierced, swords hewed, and arrows struck their target.

Gwen's first thought had been for the bird on her wrist. Slipping off its hood, she released the gyrfalcon so it could fly to safety. Only then did she discover the full measure of Faerie's blessing and her wondrous transmutation.

There was a moment's blur in which she felt the giddy thrill of flight. Then flashed an onslaught of images. A bird's-eye view of the battle scene clashed with her own ground-level perspective. She was in her body where it stood, but she was also inside the falcon as it soared into the air.

"It's me!" she shouted, lifting her spear.

"It's me!" she screeched, as she dove from above.

Caught off guard by the Company's audacity, the Hunter was slow to rally and retaliate. Numerous wounds were inflicted upon him. His roars bellowed through their minds. His sight darkened as countless eyes were destroyed. He lost a hundred to Katie's arrows alone, before he lunged down at her.

With one sweeping gesture, like the crack of a whip, he dashed her against the rocks.

She crashed to the ground with a scream of agony. Crom Cruac moved to strike again.

Mattie rushed to Katie's side and dragged her out of the way, behind the rocks. Her limbs looked twisted and wrong. Blood stained her clothes.

"Oh God, your legs are broken!"

"Prop me up," she gasped. "My arms are good."

"You're wounded. You need—"

"There's no time for nursing!" she cried. "If we stop, all is lost!"

Eyes wet with tears, Mattie did as she told him, wedging her battered body between two large stones.

She tried to smile through her pain to comfort him.

"It takes more than one swipe to beat a redhead."

And once more the archer let fly her arrows.

Mattie returned to the combat, enraged with a frenzy

that sought revenge for Katie's wounds. Each thrust of his lance struck with ruthless fury.

The blow to Katie taught the Company a lesson. They changed their tactics. In a dance of death they advanced and retreated, now striking Crom Cruac, now running from his blows.

Maddened, the Worm came out of the lake and coiled upon the shore. Huge and swollen, he rolled toward them to crush them beneath his weight.

But their smallness was an advantage. They scattered in all directions, only to regroup on the other side to charge him again.

Though she fought well on foot, it was Gwen's attacks from the air that did the most damage. As with all raptors, the white gyrfalcon was most ferocious in female form. The darling of kings and emperors, its persistence was legendary. This was a creature that never gave up. She swooped with deadly aim, beak and talon tearing at her prey.

Strengthened by the grace of Faerie, Granny fought like a warrior. She had been using her staff as a spear before she learned, to her delight, that it discharged bolts of fire. Then she wreaked more havoc upon the Hunter.

Though Dara saw that his great-aunt had power, he fought alongside her in a protective manner. He also kept watch on Gwen wherever she battled. It may have been this divided attention that caused him to falter, with dire consequence. For he was the one who discovered the ultimate horror.

After piercing a great eye that loomed above him, he retreated too slowly. A viscous fluid splashed onto his arm, searing the flesh to the bone. He staggered back in shock and pain, and shrieked a warning to the others.

But his cry came too late.

Wielding two swords simultaneously, Findabhair slashed and hewed. She fought with a fierce passion, aware that her friends were suffering on her behalf. But despite her swiftness, the Worm landed a blow and beat her to the ground.

Something broke inside her, she felt it instantly. She couldn't move. As the darkness gathered around her, she saw the eye that mirrored her death. Then she heard and saw no more.

Finvarra had been striking from the air when he spied Findabhair's plight. He flew to her side, but she lay unmoving. He placed his shield over her even as Crom Cruac lunged to deal a final blow. With sword and spear Finvarra kept him at bay, striking again and again.

The furious assault was too much for the Hunter. The stinging blows too many. He retreated from Finvarra, but not before ruin had been wrought upon his enemy.

Standing before Findabhair to protect her, Finvarra couldn't escape the poisonous rain of the eyes. His wings were set ablaze. Too shocked to cry out, he dove into the black water. When he crawled out again the flames had been doused, but the wondrous appendages trailed behind him like rags. His eyes were glazed with anguish. In his immortal life, he had never known pain.

"Retreat!" cried Gwen. Her cries came from above and below. "To the rocks near Katie! There's a cave. Retreat inside!"

The keen sight of the falcon had spotted the cleft in the rocks. Now the Captain of the Company of Seven shouted new orders from her vantage point. Granny was to distract the Hunter with flashes of fire. Katie was to shower him with the last of her arrows. Under this cover, the others would withdraw.

Mattie ran to lift Findabhair in his arms, to carry her to safety. Gwen reached Finvarra who swooned against her. Dara was close behind, clutching his ravaged arm. He tried to help Katie. In a feat of sheer will, she was dragging herself over the rocks to join them. One by one the Company crawled through the cleft where the Worm couldn't follow.

The cave was dank and dark, but there was room enough to move. Granny was the second-last to arrive, still firing from her staff. Last of all came the royal gyrfalcon, reluctant to withdraw even at the end. She perched on a narrow ledge above Gwen's head.

A dismal silence settled over the Seven, broken only by the moans of the most wounded. Granny tore cloth from their garments to make bandages. No one was unscathed; all were battered and burned to serious degrees. But there was one who had injuries beyond the rest.

Gently the old woman laid a hand on Findabhair and stared into her eyes.

"She is dying."

Thirty-one

No, this can't be happening," said Gwen.

She gathered her cousin into her arms. Findabhair was unconscious. Gwen's tears fell freely, and her body shook with heart-rending sobs. The falcon buried her head under its wing.

Mattie stammered his bewilderment.

"This doesn't . . . It isn't . . . It's not what I . . ."

His voice trailed away. What had he expected? A glorious battle? The inevitable triumph of good over evil? Anything but this smell of burnt flesh, this distortion of limbs, these faces so tortured by suffering they were hardly recognizable. And worst of all, the cold fact of death.

Wasn't this what every soldier discovered on going to war? That it's not a grand thing, not even an epic tragedy, but something miserable and demeaning.

Katie stared sightlessly ahead of her, clenching her fists against the tides of pain. Would she die, too, in this dreary place? And for what reason would her life be cut off in its prime?

"Were we wrong, then, to challenge the universe?" Her voice sounded flat and hopeless. "Findabhair was the sacrifice. This can't be a coincidence."

Sensing the catastrophe, Finvarra struggled to come out of his swoon.

"Do not let her die!" he urged Gwen.

Gwen turned frantically to Granny.

"You have healing arts, can't you cure her?"

"It's possible," the Wise Woman said. "But I need my herbs. We must get home. Can we make it to the Black Gates?"

Looks flew around the Company with the winged speed of hope. A light was kindled in each eye. Despite the desperate state of their wounds, they would make the attempt.

The decision made, they moved with the speed of a single mind.

"I'll take Findabhair," Gwen said. "I'm strong enough. The falcon will keep watch from above."

"I'll carry you," Mattie said to Katie.

"My hero," she grinned, with a flash of her old fire.

"You can lean on my good arm," Dara told Finvarra, then nodded to Granny. "We can support him between us."

The Wise Woman agreed.

"That will leave me a free hand to work my staff."

"Let us go quickly, dear friends," Gwen said. "The last charge of the Company of Seven. Onward to the Gates!"

"To the Gates!" they echoed.

Ready for the worst, they were not prepared for what awaited them outside the cave.

There on the dark shore lay Crom Cruac, motionless. Blood trickled from gaping wounds where once were his eyes. A hint of life was still in him, but it was faint like a shadow. Slowly, horribly, he slid toward the lake. Reaching the fringe of the water, he shuddered with great spasms till he swallowed his own tail.

Then he rolled into the tarn and sank beneath the surface.

"We have won," Gwen said, dazed. "Let us take our wounded home."

There was little triumph in their progress toward the Black Gates. They were in too much pain, too weak and dispirited. The nightmare of battle still darkened their thoughts. But the urgency of Findabhair's plight spurred them on.

They were nearing the portal when they froze in new horror.

A tremor shook the still weight of the tarn, as if something huge below shuddered awake. The agitation increased, till waves slapped at the shore. As the lake convulsed, they felt its upheaval in the depths of their minds.

Up rose the Great Worm, fully healed and glistening.

Here was an Enemy who could not die.

Dare you challenge me again?

They could not be expected to rally against a newly risen foe, not one who proved to be invincible. All felt the deadening of their hearts. Wounded and broken, holding on to each other, the Company of Seven admitted defeat.

Do you surrender?

"What is your will?" Finvarra called out.

His voice was steady. Though he swayed on his feet, he broke away from the others.

As it has always been. I claim the sacrifice. A hostage must yield to me.

Katie cried out. Gwen clung to Findabhair. Dara stepped in front to block the Hunter. Mattie moved to do the same. Only Granny and Finvarra did not react.

"Why?" asked Granny.

Crom Cruac inclined his great head toward her. His eyes glittered like a galaxy of stars. His aspect was neither good nor evil. He gazed down with the disinterest of the universe itself.

Why life or why death?

The old woman shook her head.

"I accept the mysteries as they stand. It's the particulars I question. Why you? Why this?"

Do you not know me, Wise Woman of Inch?

There was something in his voice that sent a thrill through her being.

I lie curled on the branch of the Tree of Life that bears both Faerie and your world like golden apples. Two spheres, two moons that eclipse each other, one fantasy, one reality,

balanced side by side. Humanity cannot exist without its
dreams, but for any dream to exist there must be a sacrifice.

A sigh issued from Granny's throat. She had already
resolved to take Findabhair's place, and the Hunter's
words eased her mind. Having lived her life with myth
and magic, she considered this a fitting end.

No, Wise Woman, it is not you I take. He knows who
comes with me. For the affront of battle, I demand more
than a human. Only an immortal will satisfy me now.

Finvarra stepped forward. He had already sensed the
Worm's appetite and knew what it meant.

There was no time for farewells, no parting caresses for
friends or beloved. The darkness had gathered around him
to stake its claim. He had to go. Drawing himself up with
the last gasp of his strength, he waded into the water.
Behind him trailed the ragged wings of a fallen angel.

There was nothing his companions could do. All
were frozen in their place by the mesmeric stare of the
Worm. Helplessly they watched as Finvarra went further, slipped deeper, into the depths of the dark water.

Sensing her love's doom, Findabhair struggled to
consciousness. A cry tore from her throat, high and wild
with grief.

"Let me die with him!"

But like the dark of night itself, the Hunter was oblivious to her pleas. Silently Crom Cruac sank beneath the
waves.

And so, too, did Finvarra, King of Faerie.

Thirty-two

How long they stood in that netherworld of despair they couldn't be certain. The change that took place was as slow and subtle as the arrival of dawn. It was the absence of pain they registered first. Their injuries had vanished, leaving them fully restored. They were also back to their normal selves. With a pang, Gwen felt the loss of her falcon.

Then, as the morning light unveiled the landscape, they saw where they were. To their left, in the distance, rose the Knockalla Mountains. On their right was the Scalp. Ahead, across an expanse of bright water, winked the lights of Rathmullan. They were standing on the stony shore of Lough Swilly.

"We're on Inch," Dara uttered at last. "At the old fort."

Granny looked gray and defeated. Her voice quavered as she spoke.

"The hostage yielded. The sacrifice was made. The night of the Hunter's Moon has passed."

There was no joy in finding themselves safe and returned to their world. Each suffered the deep wound of the loss of the King. Their Company was riven, their circle broken. It is difficult, indeed, to come home from the wars.

Findabhair stood cold and white as a statue. Only her eyes showed the intensity of her grief. The others gathered around her to offer support, but there was little they could do. She was inconsolable.

Gently, silently, Gwen took her hand, and they all left the fort. Bowed with sorrow, they walked without speaking, down the road that led to Granny's.

The morning light was streaming over the island. Robins and blackbirds sang full-throated from the trees. The cry of a baby could be heard in a nearby house, as the smells of breakfast wafted through the air. They couldn't help but reflect that, regardless of death, life carried on.

When they reached Granny's cottage, Findabhair wouldn't go in. Waving them quietly away, she wandered alone through the wild garden, into the woods behind.

"Leave her be," the Wise Woman said. "Let her grieve him as she sees fit."

"Blessed are they who mourn," Katie whispered softly.

Deep in the woods, Findabhair found an ancient oak with wildflowers clustered at its roots. She sat down in the grass and leaned against the tree, closing her eyes. Leaf and branch sighed above her. The trailing ivy on the trunk whispered in her ear. Bees hummed in the sunshine, murmuring their secret language in an effort to soothe her. All of nature inclined toward her, for they knew the Queen of Faerie had lost her King.

In the cottage, Dara closed the curtains to signal that someone in the house had died. Katie put on the kettle for tea. Though the day was warm Mattie lit a fire in the hearth, as all of them were shivering. Death had entered their consciousness and was passing through them.

"We can't go home yet," Gwen said to Granny. "She wouldn't be able, not right away."

The old woman agreed.

"You are both welcome to stay for as long as you wish."

Like blood kin, a family in mourning, all wanted and needed to stay together, to comfort one another.

That first long day was a blur of numb pain. Meals were made and barely touched. Long silences were broken with bursts of tears. Sometimes a merciful sleep fell on one or the other, but it only meant they woke to a fresh bout of loss.

When Findabhair returned, she would speak to no one. She sat by the fire, gazing at the forget-me-nots she clutched in her hands.

It was twilight that brought the fairies. Dusk had fallen over the fields and hedgerows. The early glimmer of stars hailed the night. First came the music, quivering on the air, dim sounds so plaintive the heart ached to hear them.

Without a word, the six rose together and left the house.

Pale flashes flickered in the sky above Dunfinn. A golden light meandered down the hill, like a shining snake in the grasses. Coming into sight, the procession moved with the languid grace of those who lived in the Dreaming. Dressed in shining raiment, they walked on foot, carrying tall lanterns. Silver banners streamed behind them. Their faces shone with an unearthly light, pale and sad and beautiful.

At the head of the column walked Midir solemnly. His red-gold hair fell to his shoulders. The star of kingship glittered on his brow. Cloaked in a mantle of green leaves, he carried a golden cup before him.

Though his eyes lingered a moment on Gwen, he went first to Findabhair.

"You need not sorrow for our fallen King. Drink deep of the mead from the Cup of Forgetfulness and thou wilt be freed of his memory."

Findabhair's anguish was palpable, but there was no doubt or hesitation in her reply.

"I would rather live with the pain of his loss, than not to have known him."

Midir presented the Cup to each in turn, and one by one they graciously declined. With a low bow, he acknowledged their decision. Then he poured the honeyed liquid onto the earth.

"Nor shall he be forgotten in Faerie."

Though none partook of the Draught of Forgetting, all were blessed that night with a long and healing sleep. They awoke refreshed the next morning, able to face the day.

Mattie and Katie were the first to go. In the midst of

tearful farewells, everyone agreed to meet the next year to hold a memorial in their friend's honor. With that pledge they were strengthened, and their parting made bearable.

For many days after, Gwen stayed with her cousin on Inch. Findabhair was loath to leave the place where she had last seen her beloved. From dawn to dusk, she haunted the shores of the cold lough, searching the waters for any sign of him. Sometimes the others accompanied her, but she preferred to be alone.

At first Gwen couldn't enjoy the remaining time she had with Dara, for she felt too much grief and guilt. But Granny soon put a stop to that.

"If you fail to live your life well, you dishonor the sacrifice of our fallen comrade. It is your duty to be happy."

Thus encouraged, Gwen and Dara spent their days together as cheerfully as they could, shadowed by the loss of their friend and their own inevitable parting.

The night before she left, Gwen walked with Dara in the garden. The scent of honeysuckle perfumed the air. The moonlight cast bright shadows over the flowers and trees.

"Have you ever been in love?" she asked him shyly.

He smiled at the question.

"You mean before you?"

Their faces shone in the dimness.

"No," he said softly. "Not before you."

"And now?"

"Yes, now. You."

"I love you too."

EPILOGUE

It was a year later when they all met again on Inch
Island, a year and a day since Finvarra died. The
reunion was loud and lively at times. Katie arrived with
Mattie since her motorbike had broken down and she was
saving to buy a new one. She admitted to luxuriating in
the big Mercedes.

"It was like sitting on a sofa! I kept looking for the
telly!"

Dara drove the length of Ireland to pick up Gwen
and Findabhair in Bray. Gwen wore the golden heart that
he had sent her for Christmas. When she first opened the
door to greet him, she was so overwhelmed that she was
about to act shy. He didn't give her the chance. With a
great cry, he caught her into his arms.

Findabhair had come of age in the passing year.
There was a depth and grace to her slender beauty. She
had learned to live with the death of a loved one.

When all were gathered in the Wise Woman's cottage, they sat down together to a funereal feast.

"Granny and I have been cooking day and night for weeks," Dara declared.

He spoke with pride, and rightly so. Only in Faerie had they ever dined so sumptuously. The dinner was served in the old style of Irish feasting, with three courses or "removes" that were each a meal in itself. The first course started with a homemade soup of carrots, leeks, and fresh peas from the garden, followed by artichoke pie, buttered dulse and pickled samphire, sugared beetroots, broad beans in butter, and various salads of sorrel and herbs. These were accompanied by an assortment of breads including raisin scones, farls of wheaten, little soft white rolls, and the potato-cake dishes renowned in the region—fadge, boxty, and champ.

The second remove featured a great platter of grilled salmon and trout, eggs roasted in the turf ashes, onions baked in their jackets, fresh mountainy mushrooms fried in butter and garlic, carrageen moss as light as a sponge, and a great hill of potatoes, all white and floury, sprinkled with chopped parsley and chives.

The third course was a delight to charm any sweet tooth: almond cream pudding that melted in the mouth, an apple barley flummery, hazelnut and honey biscuits, butter sticks with orange butter, tea brack thick with sultanas and fruit, and a great bowl of gooseberries, strawberries, raspberries, and black currants in a swirl of golden cream.

To wash it all down, there were bottles of elderflower

and blackberry wine, a jug of frothing buttermilk, and pots of brown tea.

"I'll have a bit of everything," said Gwen.

They ate at a leisurely pace for hours, talking and laughing. At the head of the table a chair was left empty and a place setting unused. Throughout the meal, they raised their glasses and toasted Finvarra, speaking of him as if he were there. This was the Irish way, not to deny death but to acknowledge it, and to celebrate in the name of the one who had gone.

Shortly before twilight, they set out in procession down to Inch Fort. Dressed in their best clothes, solemn and silent, each carried a candle and a death gift to honor him.

The dusky light of evening fell like a mist on the fields. The road was a gray ribbon wound around the island. In the distance, the dark mountains stood watch on the landscape.

When they reached the stony shore of Lough Swilly, they lit their candles. One by one they offered their gifts to the deep of the lough.

"Not all that is gone is gone forever," said Granny, as she slipped the silver ring from her finger and dropped it into the water.

"All kings and princes bow to the High King," were Dara's words, as he watched the crown of oak leaves float away.

From her knapsack, Katie took out a bow and arrow.

As soon as she lit the kerosened point, she stepped back to aim.

"You were a wonderful dream," she whispered.

The fiery arrow arched over the dark lough, then plummeted into the water like a falling star.

"My king, my king," said Mattie.

There was a flash of gold as the coin spun against the sky before diving down.

"You were an enemy, and then a friend," Gwen said quietly. "Thanks to you, I learned to be strong."

The bouquet of buttercups was twined with the briar of a wild Irish rose.

It was Findabhair's turn. The others watched sadly as she walked to the edge of the drear lake.

"I return the gift you gave to me," she said softly.

As she reached out to the waters, they saw her hands were empty. Then she began to sing.

'gCluin tú mo ghlór 'tá ag cur thuairisc
Ó mhaidin go nóin is as sin go deireadh lae?
Éist, a stór, tá ceol ar an ngaoth
Is casfar le chéile sinn roimh dhul faoi don ghrian.

Do you hear my voice that's asking for you
From dawn till noon and then to day's end?
Listen, my love, music is on the wind
And we will meet before the sun goes down.

Tears sprang to their eyes. As soon as they heard the beautiful song, they knew. Findabhair had not left Faerie empty-handed. She had been given the gift of *ceol-sídhe*, the power of fairy music.

Shiúlas i bhfad is do shamhail ní fhaca
Ba mhór e mo bhrón is ba mhinic mé faoi néal
Éist, a stór, tá ceol ar an ngaoth
Is casfar le chéile sinn roimh dhul faoi don ghrian.

Long I walked and saw not your image,
My sorrow was great and my sky often dark,
Listen, my love, music is on the wind
And we will meet before the sun goes down.

There was an awkward moment, just before they left, when everyone paused, as if something were still to be said or done. No one expressed it, but the shadow of disappointment cast a gloom over all. They had half-expected the fairies to come. Hadn't Midir promised that the fallen King would not be forgotten?

Gwen put her arm around her cousin in silent support.

"They are not like us," Findabhair murmured.

It was on their way back to Granny's, as they approached the crossroads, that they heard the music. High notes quivering on a current of wind. Skipping over field and mountain. A dancer leaping!

An impossible tune by a master fiddler.

And when they all raced breathlessly toward its source, there he was, standing tall in the grasses at the side of the road. Dressed in faded jeans and a white shirt that glowed in the dimness, he played his fiddle like a man without a care in the world. His skin was nut-brown, his feet were bare. He had the same features, finely chiseled and exquisite, but he looked younger somehow and more approachable. The sloe-black eyes shone with a genial light.

It was Finvarra, they had no doubt, yet he looked at them without recognition.

Findabhair drew near, staring at him with disbelief, too overwhelmed to speak.

He put down his instrument, and smiled at her.

Granny stepped forward.

"Dear King, are you well?"

He seemed bemused by her greeting.

"I think he has lost his memory," Findabhair managed to say at last.

"I know you are my friends," he said. Then he added playfully to her, "And *you* are special to me. Are you not, Beloved?"

She didn't know whether to laugh or cry.

"Will you come with us?" Granny asked gently.

"Of course," he replied. "I have nowhere else to go."

The others exchanged glances at this remark.

"I beg your patience, friends," he said, "but this is all

so new and strange to me. The first day of my life that I hold in my memory. Who I am or where I come from, I do not know.

"Like a newborn babe I awoke in the gloaming, on a high hill, under a hawthorn tree. I was not alone, but surrounded by many creatures—birds, field mice, foxes, and hares. There were people, too, but not like yourselves. A little man with pointed ears, an old woman in a black shawl, and a tall red-haired lad with a star on his brow accompanied by many beautiful women. They were all weeping and lamenting. It was their cries that woke me.

"'Why do you mourn on such a fair evening?' I asked them. 'Have the stars fallen? Does the moon hide her face?'

"Though none would answer my questions, they led me here. I was told to stay here till six would come. You were my friends, they said, who would help me begin my new life. Then all wept again as they took their leave of me.

"I pitied them greatly, to be so burdened with grief. I kissed each warmly and bade them be glad. For even as day must follow night, sorrow will ever give way to happiness. Is this not the truth?"

But now Finvarra saw that they, too, had tears in their eyes.

"Crom Cruac took his immortality," Gwen murmured to Katie.

"He's one of us now," her friend nodded back.

Though each was aware of the great loss that had befallen the King, they could not help but be overjoyed that he was alive and returned to them. Findabhair's heart overflowed just looking at him, her beloved whom she thought she would never see again.

"You will explain this mystery to me, I hope?" Finvarra asked, regarding each in turn.

Six smiles shone through the tears as they agreed.

"A bit at a time, I think," said Granny. "For your own sake and the adjustments you will have to make."

"You're beginning the adventure of life as a man," Mattie told him.

"It's not so bad," Dara added with a grin.

"Do you remember anything?" Gwen asked him.

She was holding Dara's hand. Finvarra frowned.

"I think of you with some affection. Are you my love also?"

"*NO!*" came the answer from three at once—Gwen, Dara, and Findabhair.

With peals of laughter and lighter step, the Company of Seven strolled down the road on their way back to Granny's. Findabhair and Finvarra drew closer together until they walked with their arms around each other. They looked no different a young couple than Gwen and Dara, who were linked the same way. Though they eventually discussed their plans to go home, all knew they would meet again and again. For the six "older" humans were well aware that a new life had been entrusted to their care.

And when the Company passed the Fargan Knowe, a wind suddenly gusted through the stand of trees. Leaves and small stones eddied in circles, rattling over the ground like the scamper of feet. A whisper sighed on the air.

The King passed by. Long live the King.

Glossary

Key to Pronunciation
and Meaning of Irish Words

Aengus Óg (en-gus ogue)—Aengus the Young, the Celtic God of Love, son of the Dagda, "the Good God" (so called not because he was good, but because he was good at everything).

aisling (ash-ling)—vision, vision poem

amadán (om-ah-dawn)—fool

An Craoibhín (awn cree-veen)—little branch, twig

An Óige (on oy-ga)—*Óige* means "youth" (plural). *An Óige* is the Irish Youth Hostel Association founded in 1932, with thirty-four hostels around Ireland available to individuals, families, and groups.

Áras an Uachtaráin (ar-uss awn ukk-ta-rawn)—abode or habitation of the President of Ireland, situated in the Phoenix Park, Dublin.

a stór (ah store)—My darling (literally "my treasure")

Banshee (baan-shee)—Anglicized version of *Bean Sídhe* (baan-shee), literally "fairy woman." In Irish folklore, the banshee is a specific kind of female spirit, usually green with long hair. She follows certain families, and will howl at night outside the door (while combing her hair) if someone in the family is about to die. Though terrifying, the warning is considered a favor as it gives everyone a chance to prepare for death. However, they don't know who will die . . .

Bí ar shiúl! (bee err shool)—Begone!

bodhrán (b'ow-rawn)—hand-held drum, usually made of goatskin and wood, beaten with a small wooden stick. "The heartbeat of traditional Irish music."

Brugh na Bóinne (brew nah boyne)—*Brugh* is a literary term for "mansion" or "dwelling" and *na Bóinne* means "of the Boyne," referring to the Boyne River where the ancient mound stands. The eleventh-century *Book of Lecan* says, "The Dagda built a great mound for himself and his three sons, Aengus, Aed, and Cermaid. It was upon these four men that the men of Erin made the *Síd of the Brúg*."

Busáras (buss-ar-us)—Central Bus Station, Dublin

Cáin Adamnáin (coin add-uv-nawn)—The Law of Adamnán (chief biographer of St. Patrick), believed to have been passed in 697 A.D. Also called "The Law of the Innocents," it forbade the killing of women, children, and clerics in wartime. Declaring all of these "noncombatants," it effectively banned warrior-women and warrior-monks, both of whom existed up to this time.

Caitlín (kawt-leen)—Irish for Kathleen. To use the Irish version of someone's name would be both a formal courtesy and personal or affectionate at the same time. A subtle gesture worthy of a king.

céilidh (kay-lee) music—lively Irish music played by *céilidh* bands, usually for set or country dancing. *Céilidh* is a variant spelling of *céilí*.

ceol-sídhe (kee-yole shee)—fairy music

> '*gCluin tú mo ghlór 'tá ag cur thuairisc*
> *Ó mhaidin go nóin is as sin go deireadh lae?*
> *Éist, a stór, tá ceol ar an ngaoth*
> *Is casfar le chéile sinn roimh dhul faoi don ghrian.*

> *(Gloon too m'glorr tawh'g car h'yur-ishk*
> *Oh waw-jinn goh new'n iss aws shinn go jeer-uh laoy*
> *Ay-sht, ah store, taw kee-yole air awn n'y'aoy*
> *Iss kass-fer leh kay-leh shinn riv yull fwee dawn knee-un)*

Do you hear my voice that's asking for you
From dawn till noon and then to day's end?
Listen, my love, music is on the wind
And we will meet before the sun goes down.

Shiúlas i bhfad is do shamhail ní fhaca
Ba mhór é mo bhrón is ba mhinic mé faoi néal
Éist, a stór, tá ceol ar an ngaoth
Is casfar le chéile sinn roimh dhul faoi don ghrian.

(H'yoo-liss ah wawd iss doh h'yowl nee aw-cah
Baw worr ee moh vrown iss baw vinick may fwee neel
Ay-sht, ah store, taw kee-yole air awn n'y'aoy
Iss kass-fer leh kay-leh shinn riv yull fwee dawn knee-un)

Long I walked and saw not your image,
My sorrow was great and my sky often dark,
Listen, my love, music is on the wind
And we will meet before the sun goes down.

Song: *Éist, A Stór,* by Máire ní Breatnach

Cnoc na mBan-Laoch (kuh-nock nah mawn lee-ock)—
Hill of the Women-Heroes

craic (krack)—Conversation, chat, but now generally means "fun." Often used with *ceoil* (kee-ole), "music," as in *craic agus ceoil.*

Críode na Boirne (kreed nah borne)—Heart of the Burren. *Críode* is a variant spelling of *croí*, meaning "heart."

curcudgellach (cur-cudge-eh-luck)—Anglicized word for "affectionate" used on Inch Island. Possibly from Scots Gaelic.

Daire (deer-uh)—Male name, from *doire* (deer-uh) meaning "oakwood." Also *dair* (deer) meaning "oak."

Feis (fesh)—This word has many meanings in both Old and Modern Irish, including accommodation and entertainment for the night, sleeping together, marriage, and even sexual intercourse. Nowadays it usually means "festival," an evolution from the *Feis Teamhrach* (fesh towr-uck)—the Tara Festival—originally held to celebrate the coronation of the High King who was ritually wedded to the sovereign goddess of Ireland, *Eriú*.

Fír Flathemon (fear flaah-heh-mawn)—Old Irish meaning "Prince's Truth" or Truth of Sovereignty.

Fóidín mearaí (foy-jeen mar-ee)—Meaning a "sod of bewilderment" or a fairy sod, i.e., ground on which one is led astray, thrown off track or into confusion.

Fulacht Fia (foo-lockt fee-ah)—Term used for the

ancient cooking pits found in various parts of Ireland.
Often a ring of stones surrounds a dip or trough in the
earth, and archaeologists have found evidence of commu-
nal feasting, such as scorched stones and animal bones.
Some believe that the gatherings in these places were rit-
ualistic, with meals being only a part of their purpose.

girseach (geer-shuck)—young girl

Gread leat! (graad laat)—Begone! (Literally, "be off with
you.")

inis (in-ish)—island

Is glas iad na cnoic ata i bhfad uainn (iss glaws ee-ud nah
kuh-nick wawd oo-in)—literally "far away hills are
green," i.e., the equivalent of the English saying "the
grass is always greener on the other side."

Magh Abhlach (mawh aw-v-lawk)—Plain of the (many)
Apple Trees (another name for Faerie)

Maher Buidhe (maw-hur bwee)—The Yellow Meadow.
Irish farmers tend to name their meadows and fields,
reflecting their personal relationship with the land.
Maher is an anglicized version of *machaire* (mock-arr),
meaning "plain" or "field." *Búidhe* is a variant spelling of
buí, meaning "yellow."

Máire Ruadh (moy-ra roo-ah)—Red-haired Mary is a historical figure of the County Clare who married three times. Her first husband died young and left her a rich widow, her second husband was killed in the Cromwellian Wars, and her third husband was a junior officer in the English army. Through the last marriage she secured her eldest son's inheritance. *Ruadh* is a variant spelling of *rua*, meaning "red-haired." *Máire*, often anglicized to Maura, is Irish for "Mary." In the Irish language, Mary the Mother of God has her own name, *Muire* (murr-ah), used by no other women called Mary.

Maitiú (maw-t'yu)—Irish for Matthew (see note concerning *Caitlín*)

Manaigh Liath (mawna lee-ah)—The Gray Monks, also called the White Monks, are the Cistercian Order, so called because their habits were made of unbleached wool of a grayish color. Despite Gwen's fears, they would not have burned her as a witch. There were few witch trials in Ireland, less than a dozen over the centuries between the first in 1324 and the last in 1711. Curiously, with the exception of the first, all the trials were of Protestants by Protestants.

Meitheal (meh-hull)—working party

Mná na hÉireann (muh-naw nah heer-inn)—"Women of Ireland" was an expression used when referring to the first female (and feminist) President of Ireland, Mary Robinson, and here extended to her successor, President Mary McAleese.

Mo chara (moh har-ah)—My friend (the possessive gives it the sense of "my dear friend" or "my dear one")

Nach breá an tráthnóna é, a chailín (nawk braw awn trahno-nah ey, ah haw-leen)—Isn't it a fine afternoon/evening (up to nightfall), my girl?

Ochón (aw-kone)—Alas!

Ochón ó (aw-kone oh)—Woe is me!

pisreog (pish-rogue) or *piseog*—charm or spell

Ráth na Ríogh (raw'h nah ree)—Fort of the Kings. *Rath* is now commonly used as an English word—without the accent—for the ancient hill forts and mounds that dot Ireland.

Rurthach (rur-haw'k)—Old Irish name for the River Liffey

seisiún (seh-shoon)—short for *seisiún ceoil* (seh-shoon kee-ole), an Irish music session, usually held in pubs and often impromptu.

Sídhe (shee)—plural word meaning "fairy folk." It is understood that the word is related to the Old Irish word *síd* used for a mound or hill-fort, in which the fairy folk are said to dwell. *Sídhe* is a variant spelling of *sí*.

Sídhe Gáire (shee gy-ruh)—The *Sídhe* are the fairy folk, while *gáire* is the verb "to laugh."

skeog (skee-ogue)—Anglicized word used on Inch Island for a fairy thornbush or tree. Provenance uncertain—perhaps from *síog* ("fairy")? Or possibly from Scots Gaelic as that language was widely used in the province of Ulster along with Irish Gaelic.

Sláinte (slawn-cha)—Health. In a toast, the word means "good health to you" or "here's health to you."

Slán go fóill (slawn go foyle)—So long (literally "safe yet")

Slievecarron (shleeve-care-un)—"slieve" is the anglicized version of *sliabh* meaning "mountain" while "carron" is taken from the Irish word *carn* meaning a "heap" or "pile," Anglicized to "cairn" and referring to a mound of stones, and sometimes to the stone mounds that are chambered tombs.

súil (sool)—eye

súileach (sool-uck)—Eyed or eye-like. Note: St. Columcille was said to have killed a monster with several hundred eyes in a pool where the Swilly River rises beyond Letterkenny, County Donegal.

Súiligh (soo-lee)—Variant of *súile* meaning "eye." In this case the word as been Anglicized to "Swilly."

Tá do ghruaig chomh fionn le ór agus do shúile gorm chomh le loch (taw doe roo-ug c'hoe fee-un leh orr awguss doe hew-leh gurr-um c'hoe leh lock)—Your hair is as fair as gold and your eyes as blue as the lough.

Tánaiste (tawn-ish-tuh)—Tanist, second-in-command, heir presumptive; in modern Ireland this is the title of the Deputy Prime Minister.

Taoiseach (tee-shawk)—leader, chief, ruler; in modern Ireland this is the title of the Prime Minister.

Teach Míodchuarta (chalk mee-ud-hurt-ah)—Banquet Hall (literally "middle round house")

Teamhair na Ríogh (tower nah ree)—Tara of the Kings. *Teamhair* means "a place from where there is a wide view." *Ríogh* is a variant spelling of *rí*, meaning "king." Author's note: Though Tara has been the sacred center of Ireland for over two thousand years, there are plans underway to run a motorway through it. See www.taraskryne.org.

Tír na nÓg (teer nah nogue)—The Land of the Ever-Young (Paradise or Faerie)

Tír Tairngire (teer torn-geera)—The Land of Promise (Paradise or Faerie)

Note on the Irish Language

The historical speech of the Irish people is a Goidelic Celtic language variously called Gaelic, Irish Gaelic (as opposed to Scots Gaelic), and Erse. In Ireland, it is simply called the Irish language or "Irish." For over two thousand years, Irish—Old, Middle, and Modern—was the language of Ireland, until the English conquest enforced its near eradication. Today it is the official first language of Eire, the Irish Republic. Recently it has been awarded official status in the Six Counties of Northern Ireland through the Good Friday Agreement.

As a native language or mother tongue, Irish is found only in a number of small communities called *Gaeltachtaí*, located chiefly on the west coast of Ireland. Sadly, these communities are declining due to economic factors, reduced rural population, social disintegration, intermarriage with non-native speakers, attrition, and immigration of non-native speakers, and the settling of non-native speakers in the areas. Some estimates put the demise of the *Gaeltachtaí* within the next few generations, a loss that would be of incalculable magnitude to Irish culture and society. It must be said, however, that native speakers ignore these rumors of their death with characteristic forbearance.

Meanwhile, the knowledge and use of the Irish language is increasing among the English-speaking population of the island. In the most recent census of 2002 (preliminary results), over a million people in the Republic and 140,000 in Northern Ireland reported having a reasonable proficiency in the language. Census figures for the use of Irish continually increase. Globally, study groups and language classes are popular not only among the diaspora—those Irish and their descendants who have emigrated throughout the world—but also among non-Irish peoples such as the Japanese, Danish, French, and Germans. In the United States (*Na Stáit Aontaithe*), language classes are available throughout the country, while the Internet lists countless sites that teach and encourage Irish.

Back home in Ireland, the grassroots phenomenon of *Gaelscoileanna*—primary and secondary schools teaching in Irish—is widespread and rapidly growing, despite tacit resistance from successive Irish governments. These schools guarantee new generations of Irish speakers whose second language is fluent Irish. The longstanding Irish-language radio station *Raidió na Gaeltachta* continues to broadcast from the viewpoint of native speakers, while the new television station *Teilifís na Gaeilge* (TG4) caters to both native and second-language speakers. Many institutions both private and public support the language, the most venerable being *Conradh na Gaeilge (www.cnag.ie)*.

There are several dialects within the Irish language which express regional differences among the provinces of Munster, Leinster, Connaught, and Ulster. Also extant is Shelta, the secret language of the Irish Travelers (nomadic people who live in caravan trailers), which weaves Romany words with Irish Gaelic.

In whatever form, long may the language survive. *Gaeilge abú!*

About the Author

O.R. Melling was born in Ireland and grew up in Canada with her seven sisters and two brothers. As an adolescent, she was a champion Irish dancer and competed in many American cities. At eighteen years old, she hitchhiked across Canada and down to California where she lived for several months. As an Officer Cadet in the Canadian Naval Reserve, she worked her way through university, achieving a B.A. in Celtic Studies and Philosophy and an M.A. in Medieval Irish History. "To travel hopefully" is her motto and she has visited such faraway places as Malaysia, Borneo, India, Denmark, Outer Hebrides, Alaska, and Canada's Northwest Territories. To date, her books have been translated into Japanese, Chinese, Russian, Slovenian, and Czech. She lives in her hometown of Bray, County Wicklow, Ireland, with her teenage daughter, Findabhair. Visit her Web site at www.ormelling.com.

This book was designed by Jay Colvin and art directed by Becky Terhune. It is set in Horley Old Style MT, a Monotype font designed by the English type designer Robert Norton. The chapter heads are set in Mason, which was created by Jonathan Barnbrook based on ancient Greek and Roman stone carvings.

Enjoy this peek at the second book in O.R. Melling's
The Chronicles of Faerie,
The Summer King

That night, Laurel had a dream. She was standing on the dunes looking out over the sea. The silver stars were reflected in the water, which lay still as glass. A faint music rose in the east and lingered like sunrise in the dark shadows of Minaun, music so soft and plaintive it made her heart ache. The sweet cadence seemed to echo the sorrow of an exiled spirit, recalling vague memories of a hapless love, or the loss of a home so far away.

White lights like candles moved over the cliffs and across the pale strand of Trawmore. As they drew closer, she saw the cavalcade of bright lords and ladies, tall and shining and blindingly beautiful. Some rode on palfreys of white and gray. Others walked with such grace their feet barely touched the ground. Flags and gonfalons fluttered above their heads. Lanterns glittered with the light of the moon. Their names were whispered on the wind and over the water. *The Still Folk. The Noble Ones. The People of the Ever-Living Land. Na Daoine Maithe. Na Daoine Sídhe.* The music surrounded them as they went, and they sang together.

Níl sé 'na lá, níl a ghrá,
Níl sé 'na lá, na baol ar maidin,
Níl sé 'na lá, nil a ghrá,
Solas ard atá sa ghealaigh.

It is not yet day, it is not, my love
It is not yet day, nor yet the morning,
It is not yet day, it is not, my love
For the moon is shining brightly.

As she looked upon them, Laurel was overcome with a yearning that pierced her heart. Her eyes welled with tears. Here was a race that would never know the weight of human life. They seemed so slight and insubstantial, so fragile and precious. The dream at the end of life's heartbreaking journey. She felt a great longing rise up inside her, the desire to protect them, to keep them safe.

At the head of the column strode a tall young man with a glittering star on his forehead. He was dressed in black like the night, and a silver mantle swirled behind him like mist. His red-gold hair fell to his shoulders. His eyes were solemn and wise.

Laurel knew without being told that this was Midir, the new High King of Faerie. She bowed her head. When she looked up again, the cavalcade was gone and a young man stood before her in black jeans and T-shirt. His red-gold hair was tied back in a ponytail. The bright blue eyes were warm and friendly. Only the star on his forehead told of his kingship.

She thought of bowing again but changed her mind. He looked her own age. She was surprised, then, when he bowed to her.

"I wish to thank thee for what you are doing for my country and my beloved."

"Your beloved," she echoed, with a pang.

She knew immediately whom he meant. She was surprised but not surprised. Hadn't Honor written that he was in love with her?

"I wished to undertake the mission myself," he said, "but I could not abdicate my duties to the kingdom. This is a perilous time for Faerie. Since the death of the First King, we are embattled on many fronts. I have yet to come into full knowledge of myself as sovereign, and I am further weakened without my tánaiste, and because there is no queen in Faerie. Where the link between the worlds grows thin, dark things are slipping through the cracks and crevices. Yet we hold back the waves as best we can.

"If you succeed in forging the Ring of the Sun, you will have saved our cause. With the bond renewed, we may heal the land and keep out the darkness, and all will be well."

"I'll do it," she promised, "for Honor *and* Faerie." Her voice rang with determination. But then her throat tightened and she couldn't stop herself from asking, "Do you know if she's all right? Would it be possible . . . Can I see her?"

Midir waved his hand over the ground between them. A pool of silver light brimmed like water. There in the depths she lay, curled up and fast asleep. *Honor.* She was like a white flower, shining and innocent, a newborn soul.

"Oh," said Laurel.

She stared at Midir with mute appeal, and saw her own pain and longing mirrored in his eyes.

"Your sister has slipped between the worlds, through one of the tears we hope to seal. When the Midsummer Fires are lit, she will awaken. Then you and I will be reunited with her."

His declaration was clear and confident, his features serene. Laurel found herself wishing for the same conviction.

"How can you be so sure?"

The blue eyes glittered like the stars above. His smile dazzled.

"I believe in you," he said, as he began to fade.

And even as Laurel surfaced from the depths of sleep, his last words dispersed like foam on the waves.

"I have always believed in humans."

Keep reading! If you liked this book, check out these other titles.

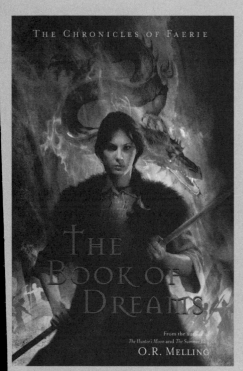

The Chronicles of Faerie:
The Book of Dreams
by O.R. Melling
978-0-8109-8346-5 $19.95 hardcover

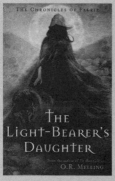

The Chronicles of Faerie:
The Light-Bearer's Daughter
by O.R. Melling
978-0-8109-7123-3 $7.95 paperback

The Chronicles of Faerie:
The Summer King
by O.R. Melling
978-0-8109-9321-1 $7.95 paperback

Visit
www.amuletbooks.com
to find out more.

Keep reading! If you liked this book, check out these other titles.

Bliss
by Lauren Myracle
978-0-8109-7071-7 $16.95 hardco‹

Fell
by David Clement-Davies
978-0-8109-7266-7 $8.95 paperback

Escape the Mask:
The Grassland Trilogy Book On‹
by David Ward
978-0-8109-7990-1 $6.95 paperb‹

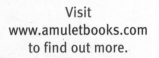

Visit
www.amuletbooks.com
to find out more.